***You think it's easy being a private eye. Well, it's not. Take the case of Sugar . . .***

The living room door opened and a small blonde, busty girl came in wearing a green belt around her waist. *Period.*

Then she turned and half glided, half wriggled out of the room. Her long blonde hair was braided in a pony tail that bumped and switched back and forth across her little rump. At the doorway she turned and peeked over her shoulder at me—then was gone.

When she appeared again, she was wearing a different belt and nibbling at the end of a banana. She smiled at me, then trotted over to sit on her haunches at my feet . . .

***What would you have done—what would any healthy normal male have done in a situation like that??? Well, I did it . . .***

# HAVE NUDE, WILL TRAVEL

*Clyde Allison*

isbn 978-1-64720-233-0

Fiction House Press
www.FictionHousePress.com

## Chapter 1

A FUNNY THING happened to me on the way to Mr. Tamerlane's office. I knocked over a fire hydrant with a DC-3.

The only reason I bother mentioning the incident is that it succinctly (if depressingly) illustrates the three factors that seem to exert a constant, baleful influence on my life: girls, flying, and bad luck.

I'd taken Mr. Tamerlane's platinum-plated private DC-3 up for a brief workout, cruised around for an hour or so, then brought her down through the San Fernando smog to make a snappy three-point landing at Tamerlane Oil's private field. No sweat. A brightly painted jeep with a FOLLOW ME sign on the back darted out and turned in front of me, and I obediently taxied along behind it towards the main hangar.

Then it was that a just-hired secretary emerged from the adjacent Tamerlane Executive Building and started trotting along on some errand. I could tell at once she was a new employee, even from the stern view she presented.

I'm extremely partial to girls' backsides, and in the month or so I'd been employed by Tamerlane Oil I'd made it a point to get as familiar as possible with every secretarial rump on the payroll.

Tamerlane Oil employed a fine selection of them, I must admit. Plump rumps and compact ones; saucy, bobbing rumps and rumps that swayed in lazy, erotic arcs like overripe fruit—there wasn't a female posterior belonging to the company that I couldn't instantly identify at fifty paces. Though I prefer to work at closer range, of course.

And this girl's rump was new to me. A pert, jaunty rump that neither bounced nor rolled but sort of switched from side to side with a happy shiver at the end of each swing. Fascinating.

Was that wanton, compound movement of her buttocks due to natural high spirits—or merely her high heels?

Engaged in such pleasant speculation I followed her closely with my eyes. Also, unfortunately, with the DC-3.

I didn't see the fire hydrant until just before I nudged it with my undercarriage. It was only a gentle nudge, but with my luck, that was enough. The tire blew, the hydrant made like Old Faithful, and the girl leaped straight up into the air with a screech.

Poor kid. I guess she thought—well, I don't know *what* she thought. At any rate, tight skirt or no, she was running fast even before her feet hit the ground. Maybe she was hurrying to get into some dry clothes.

I stuck my head out the open side window of the cockpit and watched mournfully for a few moments while people came dashing up from all directions and began running around in circles waving their arms and shouting excitedly and getting all wet. People certainly act foolishly in the least little crisis.

Then I realized that they weren't just waving their arms. They were shaking their fists. At me. From my lofty vantage I gave them a sickly grin. Then I did the only thing possible. I dashed back through the fuselage, jumped from the cabin door and sprinted like hell towards the Executive Building.

Actually, I had some excuse for hurrying: while joy riding in Mr. Tamerlane's private plane I had gotten an urgent call from Tamerlane Field's tower: I was to report to Mr. T. instantly at his office.

Looking back I guess that brusque summons had had a lot to do with my taxiing into the fire hydrant; it had made me edgy and nervous. And when I get that way anything can happen. And usually does.

The reason I was edgy and nervous was that I figured Mr. Tamerlane wanted to fire me. In person. In short, I was afraid that my Past had caught up with me.

Little did I suspect that, in fact, my Past was way ahead of me. . . . But I'm getting ahead of my story.

I darted through the imposing glass doors of the main entrance (fortunately remembering to open them first), shot up in the elevator to the third floor, and loped down a long length of corridor. Then I screeched to a halt, straightened my tie, and opened the door to Mr. Tamerlane's office.

His outermost office, I should say. A blonde, statuesque receptionist impaled me with a frozen stare.

"Jake O'Day," I said. "To see Mr. Tamerlane. Instantly."

The blonde receptionist nodded. A bold, incisive gesture that moved her beautiful head a full half inch. "You may pass, Mr. O'Day. I think He is expecting you."

"Yeah," I said. "I figured He was—I mean he was."

The blonde receptionist pressed an invisible buzzer, a visible door lock buzzed, and I passed through. To the next outer office. A redheaded receptionist this time, but she asked no questions; the jungle telegraph at Tamerlane Oil works fast. She just pressed her buzzer and I moved through the next door to the next office.

A brunette this time. I leered at her. She was a very attractive brunette. She stared back. Nothing. Nothing but the pressing of another buzzer and the unlocking of another door, this one as massive as a bank vault's but more decorative.

And then I was in Mr. Tamerlane's office. So was Mr. Tamerlane. I could see him distinctly, distant as he was, sitting behind his shiny mahogany desk that was only slightly larger than a Ping-pong table.

I slogged towards him through the ankle-deep carpet that lined his office from wall to distant wall. I didn't begrudge Mr. Tamerlane his enormous office. What the hell. If I were as big an oil tycoon as he was, I'd go in for a bit of grandeur myself.

Also, the long walk towards his desk gave me time to collect my thoughts, time to reflect on the unjust irony of the fact that I was (presumably) about to be fired from my well paying job as Mr. Tamerlane's personal pilot for all the wrong reasons, time to let my thoughts slide gloomily back to my past—to the years when I could still spell my past with a small 'p'.

Where had things started to go wrong? Since I'd already asked myself this question hundreds of times, I was able to answer myself at once: Wheat Rust, Kansas, that was where. Back in my old home town. In the soft, warm, treacherous arms of Nancy Lou.

She was eighteen and I was eighteen when we'd first walked hand in hand through the wheat fields like two innocent children. Through the fields and into the woods we'd walked, time after time. The woods where, with the innocent, eager curiosity of youth, we'd experimented with every sexual trick in the book.

Two books, in fact. We each owned a sex manual and worked our way (backwards and forwards) through both volumes alternately. Within a month we knew those books by heart. It saved time. When I got the urge to sample Nancy Lou's churning charms from an unusual angle, I didn't have to explain in detail what I had in mind—I just murmured *Page 147, paragraph two, darling*.

And Nancy Lou would roll happily over—or I would, depending upon the particular calisthenics called for.

What happy, halcyon days (and nights) those were. High school was behind me, college a full summer ahead, and I had nothing to do save pleasure Nancy Lou and be pleasured in return.

Sweet Nancy.

Darling Nancy.

Nancy of the fully packed breasts, the triphammer hips, the creamy ripe thighs.

Soft Nancy.

Passionate Nancy.

Nancy sprawled lazily on her back, her golden hair splayed out like a fan, her long arms spread wide, her strawberry tipped breasts jutting up hungrily towards me as I swan dived into her embrace.

Nancy swarming all over me in a frenzy of sweat-soaked animal lust, whimpering and moaning as she squirmed and writhed against me in frantic eagerness to trigger the pent-up passion in her, shaking and rocking me faster and faster and harder and harder.

Soft and hard, that was Nancy.

Soft breasts as big and resilient as water-filled balloons; soft buttocks that yielded so satisfyingly to my clutching fingers as I pulled her tighter to me; soft lips, soft flesh and softer words of love.

Soft and hard.

Hard teeth sinking like fangs into my shoulder at the moment of truth; hard, darting tongue that plunged again and again into my mouth; hard fingernails raking my naked back; her arms pulling me hard into the whirlpool of flesh that was her body.

What happy, timeless hours those were. How deeply I loved her—and how often.

Then the little bitch went and got herself elected Miss Automated Seed Drill. First prize: a one-way trip to Hollywood.

"You can't go." I pleaded.

"Try and stop me," said Nancy Lou. "You think I want to live in a dump like Wheat Rust all my life? Not little Nancy Lou. No sir. I'm gonna get in the movies. I'm gonna get ahead no matter *what* I have to do."

"You silly, star-struck kid," I'd told her, stroking her long golden hair. "Don't you realize what happens to beautiful, naive but voluptuous teen-age girls when they try to get in the movies?"

"You bet," said Nancy Lou. "They get tossed on the casting couch. Well, they won't have to toss me—*I'll* toss *them*. What do you think I've been working out with you in the woods for? I'll be the hottest naive teen-age girl ever to hit those parts." She patted her luscious hips fondly. "Real couch busters, these babies."

I'd stared at her. "You're joking?"

"Like hell," said Nancy Lou. "The way I figured things out, it was much smarter for me to spend this summer learning how to be a bitch in bed—and out of bed—than reading a bunch of stupid books on acting. I'll have plenty of time to learn acting once I get to be a big star."

I was numb with unhappiness. Looking back, it seems hard to understand why I took the whole thing so big. But I did. I was in love with the little tramp.

"What about me?" I groaned. "Don't you care about my feelings at all?"

"Frankly, no," said Nancy Lou. "You have some superficially attractive qualities, Jake. But deep down you're a creep."

"I'll kill myself!" I cried.

"Say!" gasped Nancy Lou. "What a publicity send-off that would be! Would you *really*, Jake? For me?"

"If you put it that way, no," I snarled.

Nancy Lou shrugged. "In that case you'll just have to go join the Foreign Legion or something."

"I will," I said. And I did.

If you want to be technical about it, it wasn't the Foreign Legion I joined but the U.S. Air Force. And I didn't so much join as get drafted. But the parallel is close.

Thus began another chapter in my past—still, you will note, spelled with a small 'p'.

I spent four years in the Air Force, and for the most part I had a ball. Flying had always appealed to me, and here was a golden opportunity to learn an easy, high paying job at the taxpayers' expense. It wasn't all easy, of course; I had some tough breaks from time to time.

Like when I achieved the distinction of being the first man ever to ground-loop a Link trainer. Or the time when I was flying an aerial tanker and came up behind the wrong plane. A good thing none of the passengers on that airliner were smoking when I poked the fueling nozzle through the DC-7's tail and began squirting jet fuel into the cabin. Or the time I almost dropped an atom bomb on Palm Springs. (*That* sure caused a lot of fuss—though I don't really see why. The bomb wouldn't have gone off, I don't think.)

But such minor mishaps aside, I had a ball. I got to do quite a bit of travelling, too. During my four years in the Air Force I visited Moscow, Paris, Berlin, Cairo, Bombay and Geneva.

Moscow, Vermont; Paris, Michigan; Berlin, Pennsylvania; Cairo, Ohio; Bombay, New York; and Geneva, Florida.

I don't know why the Air Force never sent me overseas. I asked a couple of times, but you know how hard it is to get a satisfactory answer out of military men. One colonel mumbled something about my not projecting the kind of institutional image the Air Force liked to see projected overseas—an evasive answer if I ever heard one.

The next time I asked a captain—Captain Bligh was the name—and the captain simply patted me on the head and said that when the Air Force felt I was ready to be unleashed upon the Free World, the Air Force would undoubtedly unleash me.

A fascinating character, Captain Bligh. She was about five feet two in her bare feet (and cute feet they were, too), with feathery red-gold hair, red-blue eyes (she drank quite a bit) and skin color of fresh spilt milk.

A cute, compact girl; compact little buttocks that fitted neatly into my cupped palms; compact breasts the size of juice apples but much softer, of course. Sweeter tasting, too. In fact she tasted pretty good all over, did Captain Bligh. And she was nice enough to say the same about me.

I might have been tempted to stay in the Air Force just for her sake—if she hadn't been made a major. As soon as her oakleaf came through she stopped drinking (she'd always been unhappy in the rank of captain for some reason) and stopped bedding me. Seems it was against regulations for a major to let herself be laid by anyone lower than a captain—and I was still a second lieutenant.

So I'd quit the Air Force to try my luck as a civilian. And what a mistake *that* was.

Things started out well enough. I got myself a transport pilot job with Atomco, a billion-dollar philanthropic oil company that specializes in developing underdeveloped oil nations for fifty percent of the take.

They sent me to Sidi Arabia, where most of their oil drilling took place. I was thrilled. I'm not a particularly adventurous person, to be honest. I don't mind travelling in style, but when it comes to enduring hardships in hot, nasty-smelling countries, I'd as soon get my kicks at home reading the *National Geographic*.

Nevertheless, I was excited my first day in Sidi Biji (the captial city of Sidi Arabia). I was East of Suez, treading the Sands of Araby, teetering on the brink of exotic, romantic adventure.

I was even more excited and thrilled that night. Who would have thought that Arab girls so young (and tender) could be so adept at such deliciously depraved stunts? And Sidi Biji boasted over fifty such famous infamous houses—each full of lithe, limber, licentious girls.

I decided I was going to like Sidi Arabia.

The next day I *knew* I was going to like the place—Atomco assigned me the job of being personal pilot to the sheik's brother (one of his brothers, that is—he had twelve of them), Ali Something-or-other.

The assignment didn't surprise me. I knew that oil companies in the Middle East went out of their way to butter up the local rulers. If they didn't the Arabs would call in another company.

But while I wasn't surprised, I was sort of pleased. Especially when, that very day, Ali Something-or-other (a tall, black-bearded man with a disconcerting Scotch accent—he'd learned English at the University of Edinburgh) asked me to run him down to his winter palace at Dar al Wadi: he wanted me to fly his harem back to his summer palace in the capital.

Wow! Me, a farm boy from Kansas flying a plane-load of harem cuties. How soft could a job get?

Had I but known—but of course, I didn't.

At Dar al Wadi the sheik's brother personally supervised the loading of his harem while I peered out the cockpit window watching the heavily veiled girls scuttle aboard the Convair, two by two. Forty-eight of them. A two month's supply.

It didn't take long to load the girls, docile and fast moving as they'd been, and within five minutes of landing at Dar al Wadi, I was ready to take off again. Which I did. Alone. The sheik's brother had decided at the last moment to stay overnight at Dar al Wadi. I figured he wanted to take spring inventory of the rest of his harem. Had I but known—but, as I mentioned, I didn't.

Anyhow, I took off. Alone. Alone save for forty-eight veiled chicks in the cabin behind me. What to do? It was a two-hour flight back to Sidi Biji. If I put the ship on automatic pilot I could—NO. Absolutely not.

On the other hand, *why* not? I wouldn't get fresh with the girls. Just stroll casually back to the cabin. And see how they reacted. It would be just common politeness to pop in for a moment. Make a little speech.

*Hi, girls, I'm your friendly Captain, Jake O'Day. If there's any little thing I can do to make your trip more comfortable, more memorable, just say the word. Or just wink. I'll get the message. You see girls, I—— Girls! Now girls, stop that! You'll catch cold without your clothes on . . . girls! Stop! Have you no shame? Whoa. Slow down. One at a time girls—or at least no more than two at a time. Well, three at a time if you insist. Four at a time? How in the world——? Oh. Oh yes. Oh my yes. How ingenious. Oh yes indeed. Speed up just a little, will you? That's it. Ah. Oh. Oh my. Oh zowie!*

I shook my head violently and tried to concentrate on flying the Convair. No use. Visions of harem girls danced like sugar plums before my eyes.

Forty-eight girls. Count them—forty-eight. Assorted

sizes and skin shades, most likely. A guy as rich as the sheik's brother could afford to stock his harem with imported stuff.

I stared out the windshield at the rolling sand dunes far below—and like erotic mirages, the imagined shapes of harem girls rose naked and tempting before my eyes. Arab girls with breasts like golden sand dunes tipped by the rising sun. Nubian girls with flesh like burnished ebony. Circassian girls with full, creamy thighs and swaying, fuller breasts. Ivory-fleshed girls from the Ivory Coast; Malay girls with tawny red-gold skin and saucy up-tilted breasts tipped with nipples of deep chocolate; Chinese girls, exotic eyed, lustrous haired, with breasts like golden goblets designed for a man's lips.

My lips.

And my hands and fingers and . . .

I broke off my thoughts. I *had* to. Another moment and I'd have lost all control. As it was, I was shaking so hard with excitement I was making the whole plane shake. In another . . .

The whole plane shake? Impossible. No it wasn't. The starboard engine was acting up. I switched her off and feathered the prop. I looked out at the port engine. It was spraying oil. Not so good. I looked at the map. *Drop in at any time at Madame Fatima's House of All Nations. Just turn left at the sign of the Infidel's Head and . . .* Damn. Wrong map. I tossed aside the street map of Sidi Biji and found my flight map. Ah. There was a field not twenty miles away, just across the border. Trucial Kali.

I swung the plane's nose around and headed for it. Ten minutes later, just as the port engine coughed to a halt, I rolled safely along the runway at Trucial Kali.

And that was when my Past began.

## Chapter 2

ALL THINGS CONSIDERED, I suppose I was pretty lucky in being allowed to leave Trucial Kali after spending only three months languishing in a dungeon.

I mean, I can see how the Trucial Kalians got so bugged

at me. They just couldn't believe I was as innocent as I claimed to be; they just figured I was playing dumb. And in a way I can't blame them.

After all, I *did* fly over their damn national border and land on their stupid prohibited field. With a plane load of Sidi Arabians—all armed to the teeth.

Harem girls, hell. What Ali something-or-other obviously had intended was to sneak forty-eight of his toughest soldiers into the capital so's they could knock off the sheik and make Ali the new ruler. If I'd known more about Sidi Arabian politics I'd have realized that trying to bump off the sheik and take over in his place was almost a national pastime.

I didn't know this, though. And it wasn't *my* fault that the soldiers Ali had loaded aboard the plane figured we'd arrived at the Sidi Arabian capital—and went charging across the field to capture the airport tower in the belief that it was the sheik's palace.

They captured it, too, in a blaze of machine pistols and hand grenades. But *I* wasn't helping them—I was too busy trying to get the plane's engines to start so I could get the hell out. They wouldn't start, so I hopped out of the plane and began sprinting towards the border twenty miles away.

I didn't make it. The crack Trucial Kali Army captured me just outside the airport. The crack Trucial Kali Army had been ordered to recapture the airport tower, but for the time being they were willing to settle for me. Possibly because I wasn't carrying a gun.

That was how I got thrown in a dungeon.

It was a pretty dull three months, actually. After some initial talk about boiling me in oil, they treated me quite well. Partly, they explained, because the Kingdom of Trucial Kali was noted for the kindly manner in which it treated invading swine such as myself, and partly because they didn't want me all marked up, in case they decided to ship me to the United Nations as Exhibit A.

Because if things were quiet in my dungeon, all hell was popping outside. First off, everybody disowned me. Ali Something-or other disclaimed all knowledge of my flight (naturally) Atomco Oil fired me. The State Department officially washed its hands of me. And the CIA issued a special statement denying that it had financed my invasion.

Meanwhile, in my dungeon, my polite questioning went on.

"Where iss your papers, Colonel O'Day?" (The Trucial Kalians always assumed I was a colonel—probably because that was the lowest commissioned rank in their crack army.)

"I don't have any with me. I left them in Sidi Biji."

"Ah. Very shrewd of you, Colonel. But not quite shrewd enough. You forgot that your name was stencilled on the old Air Force shirt you wore. So we know who you are. Now, who iss your boss? Colonel Nasser?"

"Certainly not."

"Ah. So you *are* one of Ben-Gurion's agents."

"No!"

"Then you *must* be from the CIA, no?"

"No. Anyway, you said the CIA disowned me."

"True. But only in second statement. First statement said you were on routine weather flying mission. A goof, no? But which statement was goof? Also, if you are not CIA man, why have three American senators denounced you for not using your poisoned needle?"

"It's election time, I suppose. Look, I'm innocent I tell you. Ask the harem girls—I mean soldiers—I flew in. *They'll* tell you I didn't know what was going on."

"Bah. How can we question them when they are still holding out in our glorious airport tower? Even our crack Trucial Kali Army cannot dislodge forty-eight hundred armed men overnight. Or even overmonth. But we will triumph, never fear. We have invoked our treaty with the accursed British and they are sending their accursed Coldstream Guard. Also two cruisers."

The Coldstream Guard arrived on schedule and stormed the airport tower. It was empty, of course. The harem girls/soldiers had long since slipped away under cover of darkness.

Which left me holding the bag.

The State Department eventually (and reluctantly) got me out by promising to build the Trucial Kalians a dam. Also a new airport tower.

Back in Sidi Biji you'd think I had B.O. or Something the way everybody avoided me. Ali Something-or-other spat on me; Atomco Oil gave me two weeks pay and my dismissal notice; and the Sidi Arabian government gave me forty-eight hours to leave the country.

The only people who loved me were the reporters. I guess I must have seemed a colorful figure to them—and their readers. The Trucial Kalians had taken my clothes, to search for poisoned needles—and then lost them in the laundry; and of course they hadn't allowed me a razor for fear I would cut my throat—or theirs.

Hence when I got off the plane at Sidi Biji I was in flowing Arab robes, with a flowing beard to match. That was when I got the nickname, "Jake of Arabia."

Also, since it was now more or less established that I hadn't invaded Trucial Kali under orders from any government, the reporters took for granted that I'd invaded at the head of my own private army, that I'd hoped to become King Jake the First, Ruler of all Trucial Kali.

Naturally this bugged me. Because even with my limited experience with civilian life I realized that airlines would not exactly fall all over themselves to hire a pilot known as Jake of Arabia. They didn't. I sent off fifty-five telegrams to fifty-five airlines—and got back fifty-five polite variations of *drop dead.*

Then, miraculously, just before my forty-eight hours were up and I was about to be deported from Sidi Arabia, a small French airline offered me a job—even sent me an advance and a plane ticket. I wired back happily that I would take any kind of job they had to offer, and hopped on a plane to Paris.

They say Paris in the spring is a beautiful city. I wouldn't know. I never left the airport. The French gave me forty-eight minutes to leave their country, and there just wasn't time to sight-see. It wouldn't have been healthy, either—not with that screaming mob of irate Frenchmen surrounding the airport.

The French police were very polite, though; even brought me late editions of the Paris papers to read while I waited for my plane to take off. I understood just enough French to make out the captions under the photographs.

Interesting photographs, too. One of me in Arab dress labelled *The American Assassin.* Another of the small French airline owner behind bars labelled *Die-hard O.A.S.*

*Terrorist Confesses Plot.* There was even a photograph of the plane he'd intended me to fly—a surplus B-26 bristling with surplus bombs and rockets.

"I'm innocent," I protested. "I wouldn't have bombed and strafed De Gaulle. Honest I wouldn't."

"Just so," said the French Police Inspector. "And this telegram you sent—the one that says, and I quote, 'No job is too despicable for me.' You did not send it, perhaps?"

"I sent it," I admitted. "But it's suffered a lot in translation."

"Just so. Bon voyage, Monsieur O'Day. You understand that if you come back we will shoot you?"

I said I understood.

Half an hour later I was in London. The English were even more polite than the French had been. If, they told me, I was seeking political asylum—why, I was welcome to stay as long as I liked. On the other hand, there was the little matter of the Coldstream Guards and the two cruisers. It had cost the British Government quite a bit of money to liberate that airport tower in Trucial Kali. Perhaps, since I was responsible, I would be willing to repay the cost in easy weekly installments.

So I took the next plane home.

Back in the States I divided my time for the next six months between dodging reporters and trying (futilely) to get a piloting job. The trouble was, every time things would quiet down, some clown would drag my name into the headlines again. Like that South American dictator in exile who issued a statement saying that if the U.S. Government didn't help him reconquer his country he'd be forced to ask for Soviet troops—or even hire mercenary scoundrels like Jake of Arabia.

He did my reputation a lot of good—the bastard.

Even the Air Force wouldn't take me back. At the end of six months I was so broke I did a stupid thing—I took a short term job as technical adviser for a TV series called *Dirk Dagger—Soldier of Fortune.* I should have known it was only a publicity stunt. I have to admit I had a lot of fun on that job—but the end result was that I was now permanently labeled as a hard-bitten soldier of fortune.

Me—who's scared of guns.

After the TV job ended I lived on unemployment insurance. Then I sponged off relatives, spending my days sitting on the beach at Santa Monica drinking borrowed beer, and brooding.

Then, a month ago, I'd gotten an anonymous postcard in the mail suggesting I apply for a job with Tamerlane Oil. I did. And, incredibly, got hired. Apparently they didn't associated J. Q. O'Day, ex-Air Force pilot, with Jake of Arabia. Not only was I hired, I was assigned to Mr. Tamerlane himself as his personal pilot.

My cup of joy slopped over. I was flying again; I was making big money. And, best of all, my Past had been forgotten.

Or so I thought until the day I got my summons to report to Mr. Tamerlane's office.

## Chapter 3

"SIT DOWN," barked Mr. Tamerlane when I reached hailing distance of his desk.

I sat down. The only available chair was a straight-backed hard chair smack in front of his desk, so that was where I sat. It was like a court-martial scene—with me on the spot.

Directly in front of me, flanked on either side by flunkies, was Mr. Tamerlane, looking a little like an amiable toad with silver hair. He scowled at me. His flunkies scowled at me.

The flunky on his left I recognized: James T. Quinn, his number one assistant—a thin, tight-lipped character with the beady eyes of an accountant.

The other character was new to me—an odd, gnome-like little man with a huge bald head and thick rimless glasses.

I cleared my throat. "You, ah, wanted to fire—I mean see me, sir?"

Mr. Tamerlane nodded. From the open window behind him came the faint sounds of watery tumult and confusion. Mr. Tamerlane glanced over his shoulder and frowned. "What the devil's that racket?"

"Some clown knocked over a fire hydrant," I informed him. I saw no purpose in being more specific than that.

Mr. Tamerlane shot a scowl at Quinn, his assistant. "Does our insurance cover that?"

"Yes sir," said Quinn. "Section fourteen, paragraph two eighty-seven."

"Hmm," said Mr. Tamerlane. "Sometimes, Quinn, I suspect you know more about my business than I do."

"Yes sir," said Quinn. "I mean, of course not, sir."

Mr. Tamerlane produced an enormous cigar and began to chew hungrily on the end, meanwhile studying me with an inscrutable toadlike stare.

"Well, O'Day," he said at last, "I dare say you're wondering why I sent for you."

I made the verbal equivalent of a shrug. An obsequious shrug.

Mr. Tamerlane ignored me. "I think you know Quinn, my assistant. This gentleman," he said, jerking his head towards the little man with the huge bald head, "is Dr. Bolingbrook. My personal psychologist."

"Is that a fact?" I said, just for the sake of saying something.

Dr. Bolingbrook's eyes gleamed. "Are you doubting my credentials young man? I'll have you know I——"

"Shut up," said Mr. Tamerlane. Dr. Bolingbrook closed his mouth abruptly. Mr. Tamerlane rose ponderously to his feet and began to pace majestically back and forth behind his desk. "I dare say you've heard many rumors and stories about me, O'Day," he said. "Especially since you've become an employee of this company. Fantastic stories and rumors." He beamed at me. "Rest assured they are all true."

"Yes sir," I said.

"People tell me I'm an American legend. And I believe them. Doubtless you have heard how, when I was but a lad of thirty-six, my father threw me out of his company and told me to make my own living—build my own fortune. And, with nothing but my two hands, my shrewd brain, and a five-million-dollar grubstake, I did just that."

"I'm happy for you," I said politely.

"And I am happy for myself. Thanks to my native intelligence, my intuitive business sense, and the favorable tax laws granted oil companies, I am now worth—uh, what is the exact figure, Quinn?"

"Nine hundred and eighty-four million, three hundred and eighty-six thousand, four hundred and twelve dollars and six cents," said Quinn.

"Precisely," said Mr. Tamerlane. "Furthermore, I am A Legendary Figure. Perhaps that doesn't mean much to you. It means everything to me. Well, almost everything. Today, Tamerlane Oil is known and feared throughout the civilized world. Tamerlane Oil——"

He went on like that for about ten minutes. I nodded politely every now and then, but I didn't bother to listen. I'd heard it all before. The first day I'd come to work I'd had to sit through eight hours of inspirational indoctrination films concerning Tamerlane Oil Company—in addition to memorizing all eight stanzas of *Tamerlane O Tamerlane,* the Company Anthem.

"——And that," said Mr. Tamerlane ten minutes later, "is why I, Walter C. Tamerlane, am a Living Legend."

"Remarkable," said Quinn.

"Quite astonishing," said Dr. Bolingbrook.

"So what?" I said. But not audibly.

"But," continued Mr. Tamerlane, "a Legend should be perpetuated. Some twenty years ago, while sitting plotting—I mean pondering—at this very desk, it suddenly occurred to me that I needed a son to carry on my name. I at once dashed home to Mrs. Tamerlane the—the——"

He turned and looked appealingly at Quinn.

"I believe Mrs. Tamerlane the seventh was the mother of your child," said Quinn.

"Precisely. I dashed home to my current wife and within a matter of moments began to lay the, uh, groundwork for the perpetuation of the Tamerlane name. The project took rather more time than I'd anticipated, but some eighteen years ago Sam Tamerlane was born."

"Remarkable," said Quinn.

"Quite astonishing—I mean commendable," said Dr. Bolingbrook.

"What a disaster," I said—under my breath. I'd met Sam Tamerlane a few times, and if I've ever seen a walking disaster, Tamerlane's pimply-faced, vacant-eyed son was it.

Mr. Tamerlane sighed. "In ten days time Sam will be eighteen. I had hoped and dreamed that on that day Sam would enter my company. I was going to start him well down the ladder—make him, say, twenty-third or twenty-fourth vice president—and let him climb up week by week until he was ready to take over the reins."

"I'm happy for him," I said. What the hell was Mr. Tamerlane wasting time talking about his idiot son for, I wondered.

"My id—I mean my headstrong son," said Mr. Tamerlane, "refuses to fit in with my plans. In fact, three months ago when I told him how I'd mapped out his life, he told me—*me,* Walter C. Tamerlane—to go jump down one of my own oil wells."

My estimation of Sam Tamerlane went up a notch.

"What is worse still," continued Mr. Tamerlane, "in ten days time—when he's eighteen—my son intends to embark upon a—a career of his own choosing."

"What does he want to do?" I asked.

"Bah!" said Mr. Tamerlane.

"Perhaps," said Dr. Bolingbrook, "you would prefer it if I explained the situation to Mr. O'Day." He turned and smirked at me through his thick glasses. "Some months ago Mr. Tamerlane approached me and asked if I would be willing to use my psychological skills to, uh, brainwash his son. I studied the situation and, uh, Sam, and concluded that any such direct approach would prove fruitless."

"Get to the point," snapped Mr. Tamerlane.

"Yes sir," said Dr. Bolingbrook. Then, to me: "As you doubtless know, it is common, very common, for adolescent and pre-adolescent males to fantasy about romantic occupations. Small boys dream about becoming firemen or engine drivers. Older boys dream about becoming cowboys or private eyes—two occupations which have been greatly and unjustly glamorized in our culture, and——"

"Get to the point!" yelled Mr. Tamerlane.

"I am getting there," said Dr. Bolingbrook, with all the bald-headed dignity he could muster. Which wasn't much. I was fast forming the opinion that Dr. B. was a quack.

"It appears," continued Dr. Bolingbrook, "that at the age of twelve young Sam Tamerlane chanced upon a copy of *Beau Geste*. He at once decided he wished to become a soldier of fortune."

I said nothing, but a chill flowed through my veins.

"At the time, his parents—Mr. Tamerlane and his current wife—naturally laughed. Now six years have passed. Sam Tamerlane is *still* planning on becoming a soldier of fortune. And it is no longer a laughing matter."

"But that's ridiculous," I said. "Nobody *plans* on becoming a soldier of fortune. Things like that just, uh, develop."

"Precisely. But apparently Sam Tamerlane is an exception to this rule. He has been studying earnestly to become a soldier of fortune for the past six years. He is suffering from what we call a mono-orientated Walter Mitty syndrome."

"You mean he's nuts?" I asked.

Mr. Tamerlane rumbled ominously. "Of course not," Dr. Bolingbrook said hastily. "Sam is merely a little, well, immature emotionally. With a severe neurotic fixation."

Just as I'd figured: Sam was nuts.

"What we have to do," said Mr. Tamerlane, "is snap the lad out of these crazy ideas—get this cloak-and-dagger nonsense out of his system once and for all. And that's where you come in, O'Day." He chuckled. "Or should I say, Jake of Arabia?"

"I'm innocent!" I protested. "I——"

I broke off. Mr. Tamerlane was beaming. Apparently he liked the idea of my being formerly known as Jake of Arabia.

Still beaming, Tamerlane resumed his pacing, leaving a small smoke screen of cigar smoke in his wake. "Of course you are, my dear boy," he said. "I was reasonably certain that your blood-thirsty reputation was not justified when I hired you. Now I'm convinced of it."

I stared at him. "You mean it was *you* who sent me that anonymous postcard suggesting I apply for a job here?"

He nodded. "Of course. We—Dr. Bolingbrook and I—need a tame soldier of fortune for our purposes. And the private detectives I've had investigating you this past month assure me that—leaving your sex life aside—you're about as tame as they come. Even scared of guns, I hear."

"That's not true," I lied.

"No matter. The point is, you seem to be just the man we want. O'Day, I want you to show my boy a good time—and then scare the hell out of him."

I shook my head. "I'm sorry, Mr. Tamerlane. I might consider scaring the hell out of your son. But giving him a good time—no. He just isn't my type. I mean, even if he was a girl he wouldn't be my type and——"

I broke off as Dr. Bolingbrook held up a chubby hand. "You fail to understand our plan. Permit me to explain the clinical ramifications."

So what the hell. I permitted him. And for the next ten minutes Dr. Bolingbrook expounded pompously. Stripped of such jargon as *dynamic social drama* and *environmental manipulation for cathartic purposes* his plan was just plain silly.

What it boiled down to was that since young Sam was determined to embark on a career of adventuring, the best thing that could be done was to supply him with a series of "laboratory controlled adventures"—and then scare the hell out of him. After which young Sam, his wild oats synthetically sown, would settle down to a career in his old man's oil company.

I thought it a pretty dumb scheme and I said so. "And even if it's psychologically sound like you say," I argued, "why go to so much trouble? Why not just scare the hell out of Sam right off?"

"That," said Dr. Bolingbrook, "would not suffice to get these adolescent fantasies out of his system. Suppose, for example, young Sam had aspirations to become a prize fighter. We could arrange for him to get in the ring with a professional boxer—and have the boxer knock the, uh, stuffing out of him immediately. But when he came to he would not necessarily be discouraged."

"Sure he would," I said. "*I* would."

"No. He would imagine himself the victim of bad luck. To continue this prize fighting analogy, it would be much sounder, psychologically speaking, to let the boy go great guns for several rounds and *then* knock the stuffing out of him. He would then decide that prize fighting was not for him—but since he *had* managed to last a few rounds, an emotional catharsis would have been achieved."

"I still say it's silly," I said. "Anyway, if the boy wants to live dangerously—why not let him?"

Mr. Tamerlane shuddered. "Let my boy meander off to Singapore or Timbuktu or some equally unsavory place? Never. At best he would catch some loathsome disease. More likely he'd get his throat cut. And then who would carry on the Tamerlane name? No, if my boy craves unwholesome adventures, I intend to see to it that he undergoes clean, safe unwholesome adventures.

"And that's where you come in, O'Day. This should be right up your alley. Weren't you mixed up with some television show for a while? Melodramatic plots should be easy for you. If not, hire a writer. Cost is no object, O'Day. I'm willing to pay you five thousand a week and all expenses."

"I'm sorry," I said, "but I—— Five thousand? Dollars? A week?"

"And expenses." He dug a fat billfold out of his hip pocket, extracted a dollar bill and handed it to me. "This is yours whether you take the job or not, O'Day. Evidence of good faith on my part. If you decide to help us straighten out Sam you'll get another bill like that every two weeks. Plus expenses. Plus a bonus of fifty thousand dollars if and when Sam agrees to devote his life to Tamerlane Oil."

I looked again at the dollar bill he'd given me. It wasn't a dollar bill. Or if it was, someone had erased George Washington's picture and substituted a mug shot of Salmon P. Chase. And added four zeros to all the ones.

I tucked the ten-thousand-dollar bill into my breast pocket casually, as if I were accustomed to being paid in larger bills, and said, "You tet I'll bake—I mean, you bet I'll take the job, sir."

Mr. Quinn pursed his lips. Dr. Bolingbrook smirked. Mr. Tamerlane beamed. "Splendid, O'Day, splendid." He grabbed my hand and pumped it up and down. "If you can make an organization man out of my id—my neurotic son—you'll have my undying gratitude, O'Day."

"And that, sir," I said, "plus five thousand a week and expenses, is all I ask."

## Chapter 4

THIRTY ODD MILES from Los Angeles there was once an enormous and fertile wooded tract of land known as Impala Valley. The enormous tract is still there, as are its fertile woods, but ever since Walter C. Tamerlane bought the place ten years ago and drove its few inhabitants out with threats and money, the place has been known as Tamerlane Valley.

In the geometric center of Tamerlane Valley stands Tamerlane Castle, a cozy grouping of imported and domestic French châteaux, colonial mansions, Moorish forts, Chinese pagodas and a castle that until last year was in Marienbad.

As California millionaire dwellings go, Tamerlane Castle is in subdued good taste. At least that's how it struck me as—three hours after I'd bowed my way backwards out of Mr. Tamerlane's office—I zoomed toward it in my battered MG-TD.

If the castle presented a pleasing prospect, however, the road to the Tamerlane estate was paved with ill-concealed bad intentions. Like, half a mile from the secondary road I'd turned off had been a sign as big as a billboard alerting me to the fact that I was on PRIVATE PROPERTY where TRESPASSERS WILL BE SHOT.

Half a mile beyond that was another sign: BEWARE OF SAVAGE RABID DOGS. Then another sign: LAND MINE AREA—KEEP IN CENTER OF ROAD. I slowed down to a crawl. A hundred yards farther along was yet another sign: ALL HOPE ABANDON YE WHO TRESPASS PAST THIS POINT. Beneath the sign was a neatly stacked pyramid of human skulls. I peered at them. Were they plastic imitations? No, they were—or had been—the property of real humans.

Still, I didn't believe for an instant that they were the remains of trespassers. Doubtless Mr. Tamerlane had bought them from a medical supply house. Then my eye fell on a small sign stuck jauntily into the eye socket of one of the skulls. ARE YOU *QUITE* SURE? asked the sign.

I felt somewhat subdued by the time I reached the main gate. The main gate was set in the main wall, an imposing structure of masonry that according to rumor—doubtless false—had once been part of the Great Wall of China.

A uniformed guard emerged from a steel turret and walked over to inspect me. He was very polite and refrained from pointing his tommy gun directly at me.

"O'Day," I croaked. "I'm expected."

The guard frowned at the photo on my Tamerlane Oil Company I.D. card, then at me. "Right. We got word you'd be coming." He turned and shouted over his shoulder. "Open her up, Herman."

From somewhere a gong sounded and the gigantic gates began to swing ponderously open. "Nice gates, eh?" said the guard. "They're exact copies of the ones they used in that old movie *King Kong*. Only ours are made out of steel. You can't miss the castle. Just keep going through the woods for a mile, then make a sharp left when you pass the Nike battery and the castle's another mile ahead."

"That," I said, "is just plain silly. Even Mr. Tamerlane couldn't own a real Nike battery."

The guard grinned. "Of course not. It's just a wooden dummy Mr. Tamerlane had built to scare away low flying planes. At least, that's what he told the Air Force people when they came around asking about a Nike battery they'd mislaid. All the same, don't get too close. The boys who man it are kind of trigger happy."

Mr. Tamerlane, I reflected as I drove through the woods toward his castle, certainly valued his privacy. I drove slowly, partly for fear of hidden land mines or tank traps, but mostly because the scenery inside the estate was worth admiring.

I don't know much about trees, but it was obvious that forests all over the world had been looted to stock Tamerlane Valley. There was wild life, too. Flocks of peacocks, all kinds of deer, and a small herd of zebra.

Then I turned a sharp curve and Tamerlane Castle lay before me, looking a little like a spare Disneyland.

I parked in front of the main building and, after a

brief hike up a flight of enormous marble steps, knocked on the door.

Silence. Aside from the distant screeching of peacocks and braying of zebras, that is.

I knocked again. Nothing. "Tell them I knocked and no one answered," I yelled. "That I——"

At that moment the door was opened by a cute little blonde-haired chick in a French maid's outfit. Both her blonde hair and her dress looked a little dishevelled—as if she'd been necking or something.

"I'm so sorry you had to wait," she said. "I didn't hear you knock at first. I was neck—talking with one of the gardeners. I don't know *where* the butler is."

"Here I am," said a tall, bleak-faced-looking butler as he emerged from a nearby door and stalked with rapid dignity towards me, straightening his tie as he came. When he got closer I noted he was sporting a large lipstick smear on one cheek.

"You must be Mr. O'Day," he said. "We were expecting you, but uh, not quite so soon."

"Evidently," I said. "If you'll pardon my mentioning it, you're not completely zipped up."

The maid giggled and scurried off while the butler discreetly turned his back for a moment to adjust his zipper.

"So kind of you to let me know," he murmured. "My name is Jeeves, sir, and——"

"Not really?" I asked.

"Well, no sir, but Mr. Tamerlane prefers to call me that and——"

"And we are all of us slaves to Mr. Tamerlane's every whim," finished a tall brunette as she emerged from a nearby door. The same nearby door the butler had just emerged from, I noted with interest.

The brunette favored Jeeves with a bland smile. "I will take care of Mr. O'Day," she said. "You may serve drinks in the library."

The butler bowed. A little morosely, it seemed to me. "Yes, ma'am. Will that be all, then, ma'am?"

That bought him another smile from the brunette. A little less bland this time. "For the time being I'm afraid so, Jeeves. Perhaps in the future you will be a little less tardy in performing your, ah, duties."

"Yes ma'am," said the butler, and plodded away disconsolately.

The brunette turned back to me and inspected me with interest. Compound interest, in fact. The expression on her face reminded me just a little of—what *did* it remind me of? Oh yes. Matilda. Matilda had been a handsome king snake I'd owned as a small boy. I'd fed Matilda live mice, and the expression on Matilda's face at feeding time had been just like—on the other hand, I could be wrong.

Not that—aside from her expression—the brunette resembled a serpent. Unless it was one that had just swallowed a life-size erotic statue.

Because this chick was like *built*. She was about twenty-eight or thirty, with long, ink-black hair that fell in lustrous ripples to below her waist. Her eyes were enormous circles of vivid green set above high cheekbones, her mouth full, ripe and passionate, her skin startlingly white.

I could see quite a bit of her skin, too. She was wearing an off-the-shoulder blouse that was not only off both shoulders but nearly off her. Only two things kept the blouse up—her port and starboard breasts.

And what breasts. Twin snow-covered peaks. Full, firm, vibrant mountains of tempting flesh. Ripe, erotic globes of taut-fleshed succulent femininity—tipped with silver-dollar-sized aureoles of delicate pink, from which rose nipples as big and red as cherries. Bigger. Redder.

(How did I know the color of her aureoles and nipples when they were still covered by her blouse? I didn't; I found out those details later. But I *guessed* that her aureoles and nipples would be a tasty pink and a passionate red, and I'm seldom wrong in these matters.)

Aside from the blouse—and her hungry expression—all she was wearing was a pair of the shortest short-shorts I'd ever seen. Usually I don't dig pants on a woman, but these pants were in a class by themselves. They were black and made out of some kind of elastic material that clung to her like wet silk.

They began low on her hips, swinging across her snow-white belly well below the navel, and they ended a tiny bit above the buttock line.

Yes. Yes indeed.

The brunette waited politely until I'd finished my preliminary inspection of her ninety percent nude body, then smiled and extended a long slender white hand, palm down.

The way she was holding it I didn't know whether I was supposed to shake it or kiss it. So I did both.

"Well, well," said the brunette. "So you're the infamous Jake of Arabia—my husband's pet soldier of fortune."

I made a noncommittal but virile grunt.

"And I, as you've no doubt surmised, am Mrs. Tamerlane. Mrs. Tamerlane the fourteenth, to be exact." She slid one arm cozily under my elbow. "And I'm forgetting my duties as a hostess. You must need some refreshment after that dreadful drive through the grounds. Let's go in the library and, uh, drink."

And with that she started striding towards the library, pulling me along with her. It was only a short walk—about thirty yards down an oak-panelled hall—but it was a memorable one. Mrs. Tamerlane (the fourteenth) had one of the widest pair of hips I'd ever had the pleasure of ogling, and with each step she took her inboard hip nudged mine in the friendliest fashion imaginable.

Meanwhile, her inboard breast was snuggled cozily against my arm. Her outboard breast wasn't snuggled against anything. It just bounced up and down cheerfully as she walked.

In the library Mrs. Tamerlane waved me into a long, deep, soft couch and poured two drinks. Then she settled herself on the other end of the couch in a graceful, erotic pose—sitting back with her heels tucked under her so that I could get a full profile view of her left thigh.

To put it mildly, it was a spectacular view. Mrs. Tamerlane (the fourteenth) was a long-legged filly, and most of that leg beneath was in her thighs. From where I sat that magnificent left thigh of hers seemed to fill my entire range of vision—a long, gleaming, dazzlingly white torpedo of flesh. Mouth-watering.

Mrs. Tamerlane (the fourteenth) smiled at me over her glass and thigh. "So you're the fellow who's going to wean Sam from his daydreams. I don't envy you your job. The poor kid's a bit of a loony, of course. Don't quote me, please."

I took a gulp of my drink and nodded, trying—with

scant success—to keep my eyes averted from the white magnet of her thigh. "Mr. Tamerlane suggested I drive out and take a look at Sam's room. Said it would give me some insight into Sam's, uh, personality."

Mrs. Tamerlane (the fourteenth) laughed. "A waste of time. Young Sam doesn't have a personality. Or a sense of humor. Or brains. And to save you a trip to the Northeast wing, I can tell you just what you'll find in Sam's quarters.

"Item. Maps of god-forsaken places with unpronounceable names. All over the walls and ceilings he's got maps. Item. Assorted guns, knives, spears, daggers and blow guns with instruction books. Item. The complete works of Eric Ambler. Ditto Edgar Wallace. Ditto Ian Fleming. Ditto E. Phillips Oppenheim. Also German, French, Urdu and Chinese phrase books. What else? Oh yes. Home study books on Judo, Jujitsu, Karate, Siamese foot fighting, and a book called *Street Fighting for Fun and Profit*. Like I said, the boy's a loony."

I nodded gloomily. "I'm afraid you're right. Still, I guess that isn't my problem. All I have to do is supply him with an Adventure. And collect five grand a week."

"What are you going to do to him—or with him?"

I sighed. "I don't know. I haven't got that far in my planning."

Mrs. Tamerlane (the fourteenth) showed her teeth in a happy, malicious grin. "Why don't you just kidnap him? Lock him up in some lonely mountain cabin or something. Spend the first week threatening to torture him. And the second week making good your threats. Then stuff what's left into a barrel along with an escape-made-easy handbook and dump the whole works into a lake."

I blinked at her. "I take it you don't like young Sam."

She shrugged. "Oh, I guess the kid isn't all that bad. Anyway, he won't be any concern of mine in a few months. I've almost finished serving my term."

"Huh?"

"Don't you know how Walt selects his wives? Seems that years and years ago he read some article which said that a girl reaches her prime at twenty-six and begins to fade at twenty-nine. Ever since then he's been marrying twenty-six-year-old girls and then trading them in for a new model three years later."

I stared at her. No longer did I have to wonder why Sam Tamerlane was a loony—it ran in the family.

"And I," continued Mrs. Tamerlane (the fourteenth) happily, "will be twenty-nine in six months. That's when I'll get put out to pasture. Tall, green pasture. With only my divorce decree and a million dollars to remind me of my days of servitude."

"Oh," I said. Evidently Mrs. T. (the 14th) didn't exactly glory in being mistress of Tamerlane Castle.

"You can think that again," she said, "if you're thinking I get good and fed up with this stinking castle—*and* Walter C. Tamerlane. I'm practically a prisoner in this dump. And all for a lousy three hundred and thirty-three thousand three hundred and thirty-three dollars a year."

She slid gracefully off the couch, stood up and stretched her arms over her head. I watched in fascination to see if the gleaming white globes of her breasts would bubble all the way out of her blouse. They didn't, but it was a near thing. Two near things.

And what things . . .

Mrs. Tamerlane (the fourteenth) set her ripe lips into a pout. "And in six months I get traded in. Like a used car or something."

She grasped the waist band of her blouse and in one sweeping gesture pulled it over her head and tossed it from her. Totally nude save for the scrap of black cloth clinging to her loins she stood smiling at me, bouncing up and down just a little on her heels so that the huge scarlet-tipped hemispheres of her breasts quivered like great erotic mounds of snow-white jelly.

Her hands moved up to lightly cup the undersurfaces of her magnificent breasts. Then she hefted them lightly. "I don't think I'm in all that bad shape," she said reflectively, bouncing her breasts up and down more vigorously. "No sag, no droop, no sway."

While she was doing this she was peering down at the gleaming white perfection of her body with an expression of detached curiosity, as if her breasts and belly and legs were things she had never seen before, things she hadn't quite figured out what to do with.

"Do you think I'll be able to find another buyer after

I get traded in?" she asked. "I've only had just the one owner—and I've been carefully maintained and used sparingly. Too sparingly."

She raised her head and smiled at me as she tugged her short-shorts down over the flaring sweep of her hips. "Though before you can make a fair appraisal," she said, "I suppose you should have a demonstration."

"That," I said catapulting myself from the couch, "was just what I had in mind."

## Chapter 5

INASMUCH AS THIS BOOK is essentially a chronicle of my efforts to cure Sam Tamerlane of his adolescent desire to become a soldier of fortune, I won't waste time swelling on the exhausting (yet stimulating) sexual interlude that followed.

It would break the continuity and interest of this case history if I spent time describing the sexual exhilaration that surged through me when I wrapped my arms around the sleek nakedness of Mrs. Tamerlane (the fourteenth) and pulled her to me.

The pneumatic ripeness of her warm, taut-fleshed breasts seemed to bathe my whole chest in fire as our bodies melded together, and my palms and finger tips seemed to buzz and crackle with excitement as I slid my hands up the milk-white plain of her broad back, then down past the warm column of her waist to trace and then cup the resilient globes of her buttocks—but such facts just aren't germane to this story, hence I'll omit them.

Nor will I take time to describe my emotions as her slender arms snaked around my neck, pulling my head down until her ripe, moist lips were mashed against mine; or the way it was when her depraved and darting tongue thrust itself deep into my mouth to play erotic games with mine.

Neither is it relevant to narrate what happened next. Strictly speaking, that is. On the other hand, since much of my life seems to consist of marvellously irrelevant things, and since I'm not always the best judge as to what is relevant and what isn't maybe I'd best hold nothing back.

Mrs. Tamerlane (the fourteenth) certainly didn't.

For a long while we stood, breast to chest, belly to belly, lips to lips; sort of warming up our engines. Then she pulled her head back a little and smiled at me, little sparks of excitement seeming to dance in her big, circular green eyes.

"You," she whispered, "have too many clothes on."

I nodded agreement and began to tug frantically at my tie. Her slender fingers closed over my hands. "Let me do it," she pleaded. "I love unwrapping packages."

So, kindly soul that I am, I let her unwrap me. It wasn't hard. Mrs. Tamerlane, Mark XIV, seemed to have a natural aptitude for undressing men. Or maybe just plenty of practice.

At any rate, I just stood stock still, sort of pulsing with anticipation, while her long, teasing fingers unbuttoned and unzipped me bit by bit.

It took her quite a while to get me fully stripped, but I didn't object. What the hell, let her enjoy herself. And she certainly seemed to be having a ball.

Every time she took off another bit of my clothing (like, say, my shirt) she stood back and beamed happily at the masculine flesh she'd exposed. Then she'd reach out to touch it, as if to make sure it was real, and then—to make doubly—sure she'd slide the tips of her fingers up and down my chest (or whatever). Up and down and around and around she slid her fingers, her touch as light as peacock feathers and as exciting as all sin.

She took off my socks last, getting down on her knees to do the job, and when she'd tossed the last of my socks over her shoulder she remained on her knees for a few moments, wrapping her arms possessively around my legs and pulling me to her, nuzzling her cheek against my stomach.

"Mine," she whispered happily, "all mine."

"You bet," I agreed. "When do you want it, baby?"

"Soon," she said. "But not quite yet. I want to get you a little more excited first. I *like* getting men excited."

"Honey," I objected, "I'm excited enough, believe me. My interest—oof!"

This last remark wasn't so much a comment as a result

of my landing flat on my back on the floor. She'd pulled my legs out from under me.

"Lie still," she commanded, crawling purposefully towards me on her hands and knees. "I'm not through playing."

So I lay on my back on the soft carpet while she played. Her idea of play being to trace teasing erotic designs over my body with the tips of her fingers. All over my body.

Her fingers slid like high tension wires over the flesh of my arms, my chest, my legs; gliding, stroking, squeezing fingers; playful, teasing, outrageous fingers that seemed to leave tracks of golden fire in their wake.

Then she retraced the route. With her lips and tongue. Her hot, full, moist lips and her hotter, more liquid tongue. It was like—well, no words can describe just what it was like. It was like being tortured in reverse; at times her thrusting tongue seemed to jab my flesh like a red hot poker, her lips like twin blow torches.

I groaned involuntarily while my body writhed and twisted under the blissful torment of her caresses.

I closed my eyes, resolved to take my punishment like a man. Then I felt my body thrill to a new, more subtle caress. Even without opening my eyes I knew what she was doing—she was bending over me to let her long, silken hair cascade over my body, then sweeping her head slowly back and forth to caress my naked body with her hair. Back and forth moved the silken waterfall of her hair, flowing in a million tingling arcs over my chest, my legs, my all.

She hadn't been kidding when she said she got a kick out of getting men excited. I was getting quite a kick out of her innocent little hobby myself.

What a talented, imaginative girl. What would she think of next? Just then I felt a firmer, warmer caress. She'd thought of something.

I opened my eyes. She was kneeling low over me and tracing little circles over my body with her breasts. She smiled at me and moved her upper body sinuously so that the great globes swayed like giant erotic fruit, their hard tips sweeping in gentle arcs over my chest.

"Like?" she murmured, raising her body a little.

"Enough," I said, "is enough. Let's stop fooling and start, uh, fighting."

Flat on her back herself now, she smiled up at me as I crawled towards her. "Fair enough," she said, and opened her long, gleaming white arms to welcome me into her embrace.

There was a soft-looking couch a few yards away, but I wasn't in any mood to waste time dragging her over to it; the floor would be good enough. I flung myself forward and down into the softness of her embrace.

As our bodies touched and then meshed she let her breath out in a savage bubbling hiss—the kind of sound a barrel of water makes when a swordsmith plunges a long, red hot blade into it, the kind of noise a killer whale makes when a harpoon is thrust deep into its vitals.

After that hiss came a moment—a microsecond—of calm. Then Mrs. Tamerlane (the fourteenth) detonated.

Detonated is the only word to describe her reaction. Her hands were clawing at my back, pulling me deep, deep into the churning maelstrom of her passion, pulling my chest down to crush—or at any rate slightly flatten—the ruby-tipped spheres of her breasts.

Her lips were bruising mine now, her tongue stabbing deep into my mouth in counterpoint to each upward lunge of her hips. I felt her long fingernails rake my back, heard her whimpering and moaning like some pain-maddened animal.

I felt her body fight me, then yield willingly, eagerly to my will as females always have and always will yield to a man who asserts himself as a man should.

I felt her fists beat against my back in a frenzy of ecstasy, felt the quivering ripeness of her legs lock around my hips to pull me to her, felt the convulsive reaction of her innermost muscles as the hard spear of masculine flesh that was my body stirred the witch's cauldron of her passion.

And then there was a thundering in my head as if a foaming torrent of liquid fire was pulsing through my whole body, and the torrent became a tidal wave of joy and I heard her scream insanely and felt her teeth dig deep into my shoulder.

Half an hour passed. A tranquil half hour.

Ten minutes to get our breath back. Ten minutes to

linger over a pair of cigarettes. Another ten to kill a pair of cold drinks apiece.

No talk.

What was there to talk about?

*Gee, I sure dig cheating on my husband.*

*Gee, I sure appreciate your cheating on your husband, who is also the guy who's paying me a big salary.*

No, talking would have been a mistake.

So we didn't talk.

We just looked at each other and smiled and said nothing.

And then we had each other again.

She fell on the couch and I fell on her and another shattering, writhing, shuddering detonation of passion took place.

It was like before.

Or maybe just a little bit better. We were a practiced team by now.

Another rest—twenty minutes this time. I was getting into the swing of things. I was getting a little pooped, though, so the third time I just lay sprawled on the couch and beckoned to her.

"This one's on me," I said.

"Oh, goody," she said. "That way's *lots* of fun."

It was. With bells on.

After that I put on my clothes and said good-bye and drove away. Sex is sex and fun is fun, but I had work to do.

Also, I didn't fancy being caught by Mr. Tamerlane. Not while he was paying me five grand a week.

## Chapter 6

THE NEXT MORNING Mr. Tamerlane fired me.

Officially, that is.

The scene was short, corny, but effective. It took place in Mr. Tamerlane's office, and it went like this:

Me: (*pushing open the door to Mr. T.'s office and slouching sullenly towards his desk*) "You wanted to see me, boss?"

Mr. T.: "Yes, O'Day, I do." (*glancing at his pimple-*

*faced vacant-eyed son*) "Sorry to interrupt our man-to-man talk, Sam, but this will only take a moment."

Sam: (*sullenly*) "Yeah. Sure."

Mr. T.: "O'Day, when I hired you a month ago as my private pilot I had every reason to believe that you were an honest, sober citizen."

Me: (*in a voice midway between James Cagney and Humphrey Bogart*) "That's me, boss. Sober and, uh, what was it you said? Oh, yeah. Honest."

Mr. T.: "Indeed? Do you then deny the truth of this anonymous postcard which came in the morning mail?"

Me: "What's it say? What's it say?"

Mr. T.: "That you are actually the infamous Jake of Arabia, the unprincipled soldier of fortune who nearly overthrew a government, almost bombed and strafed Paris, and no doubt have been mixed up in dozens of other notorious if colorful misdeeds."

Me: (*cringing a little under Mr. Tamerlane's penetrating gaze*) "Somebody squealed on me. If I get the rat that tipped you off I'll——"

Mr. T.: "You will do nothing, young man—because I'm firing you as of this moment, you crooked soldier of fortune!"

Sam: "Gosh!"

Me: (*snarling a little*) "You got me all wrong, boss. I wasn't planning on stealing your private DC-3 and using it to fly guns to a small field just outside of Guatemala City, honest I wasn't."

Sam: "Gee!"

At that moment, on cue, Mr. Tamerlane's assistant, Quinn, stuck his head inside the office door. "Can I see you a moment in private, sir?" he inquired.

Mr. Tamerlane allowed as how he could and strode—or more correctly, waddled—out of his office. First. however, he turned and snarled at me: "You wait here, O'Day. I'm not through firing you yet." With that he marched out of the office, leaving me alone with his pimple-faced—but no longer vacant-eyed—son. According to plan.

"Golly," said Sam. "Wow. Are you really Jake of Arabia, sir?"

I nodded. "Jake of Araby's the name, son—and running guns, or worse, is my game." I dived for the phone on Mr. Tamerlane's desk and dialed furiously.

"When you hear the tone," said an unctuous female voice, "the time will be ten forty-three, exactly."

I pressed the receiver close to my ear and snarled, "Put China Jones on. If he ain't there I'll speak to Singapore Louie."

"Gosh!" said Sam.

"When you hear the tone," said the unctuous operator's recorded voice, "the time will be ten forty-three and ten seconds."

"China?" I snarled. "Operation Tamerlane's blown. Yeah, you'll have to get the guns to Guatemala some other way. Yeah. Tough break for me, too. So long." I hung up.

"Golly," said Sam, whose vocabulary seemed extremely limited. "Were you really going to steal Dad's private plane and fly munitions to South America?"

I looked around furtively. "Between you and me, kid, yeah, I was. But let's not spread it around, huh?"

Sam shook his head. "I think it's a great idea. Couldn't you steal Dad's plane right now—before he gets back?"

I shook my head. "It's got a flat tire and water in the ignition. By the time the grease monkeys fix it up I'll be barred from Tamerlane Field."

"Gee," said Sam. "What a shame."

"Don't worry about me, kid," I told him. "I've already got another caper—uh, deal—lined up." I strode up and down worriedly, hands behind my back. "The only trouble is I need a partner, somebody I can trust. Where in hell can I dig up a young man with a working knowledge of Judo, Jujitsu, Karate and street fighting—preferably a guy who can lay his hands on an Urdu phrase book in a hurry? Maybe an employment agency. No, that's too risky." I paced some more.

"Sir," said Sam, "I'm your man."

"You?" I gasped, reeling back in amazement. "Surely you don't realize what you're saying. You can't actually want to be like me—a tight-lipped, fast-living, two-fisted, keen-witted rolling stone." I shook my head. "Soldier of fortuning isn't for you, Sam. It's a rough life. Piloting a fifty-knot motor launch through the blazing guns of a naval blockade . . . flying an antiquated P-51 through a curtain of ground fire to strafe defiant women and children . . . driving a tank through buildings, squashing people left and right—it's drudgery, Sam, sheer drudgery. Also dangerous."

Sam averred as how he liked dangerous action.

"Maybe," I said. "But it isn't all action, Sam. Sometimes you have nothing to do but wait. Waiting around in some palatial oriental mansion with only a few harem girls to amuse you . . . waiting in some native hut with only a native slut to keep you company . . . waiting in a sleeping bag until it's time to blow up some bridge, with most likely only some dark-eyed, full-breasted Spanish girl to keep you warm. Dull, Sam, that's what it is. Profitable, but dull."

And so it went.

After ten minutes of frantic pleading on Sam's part I finally let him convince me that he was the ideal man to help me on my next job. The dumb kid almost wept he was so happy.

"What's the job, uh, caper to be, sir?" he asked.

"Call me Jake," I told him.

"Sure, Jake. What's the job going to be?"

A good question. Aloud I said, "That depends, Sam. I've got a couple of irons on the fire right now—I'll just have to see which one heats up first. Suppose I meet you in exactly"— I glanced at my wrist watch for dramatic effect "—exactly five days. By that time things should have shaped up."

"Yes *sir,* uh, Jake!" said Sam. "How will I get in touch with you?"

"You won't," I said. "I'll call you."

And with that we parted company.

Sam, I presume, hurried back to Tamerlane Castle to brush up on his Urdu. Me, I went in search of a drink; I needed one; I only had five days in which to concoct an Adventure for Sam. And if I wanted to keep earning five grand a week for a while—with the chance of hitting a fifty grand jackpot—it was going to have to be a good one.

## Chapter 7

It was a warm, sunny day so I tooled my MG towards the beach to do my drinking under healthy conditions.

On the way I put my agile brain into overdrive and Thought.

First of all I thought what a curious irony it was that a peace-loving guy like myself kept getting mixed up with deeds of derring-do—even if imaginary. I felt really sorry for myself.

Then I remembered how much dough I was earning and felt better. After that I drove for a few miles thinking about Mrs. Tamerlane, the fourteenth. (What *was* her first name, anyway? I should have inquired.)

A curious girl, Mrs. Tamerlane; a girl destined to live in a castle away from the road. And be friendly to men. Very friendly. There was something intriguingly Gothic about the whole setup at Tamerlane Castle.

As I recalled my history, guys who built castles in the old days used to spend most of their time away from home—leaving their wives free to live it up with the hired help plus any wandering knights who wandered by. At least, that was the way things usually panned out in the old romances.

Maybe there was a moral to the whole thing. Walter C. Tamerlane had built himself a feudal castle to keep his wife in, and his wife had revived old feudal customs. What was the moral to that? I couldn't think of one. To hell with it.

Anyway, I was wasting time thinking about Mrs. T. What I had to do was think up a colorful Adventure for Sam. I thought steadily for twelve miles. Nothing.

Ridiculous. A guy with an agile brain like mine shouldn't have any trouble dreaming up a melodramatic real-life plot. I thought some more. Still nothing.

There was only one thing to do: I'd have to hire a writer.

I pulled the MG to a halt beside a roadside phone booth and dialed Mr. Tamerlane's private number.

"Sir," I said when he answered, "this is Jake of Arabia. I want to hire a writer. Okay?"

"Of course, you idiot!" he bellowed. "Don't bother me with petty details."

I thought quickly. "This writer wants four thousand a week. Is that all right?"

"Of course!" bellowed Mr. Tamerlane. "In the tax bracket I'm in, four thousand dollars is only worth forty cents to me. Government takes ninety-nine point ninety-nine percent of everything I make. Spend fifty cents if you like." He hung up on me.

I climbed back into my MG and drove on feeling a little awed. Also a little cheated. At that rate it had only cost Mr. Tamerlane a lousy dollar to hand me that ten-thousand-dollar bill. The least he could have done was slip me two or three. Still, it was too late to ask for a raise in salary now. Maybe I could pick up some fringe benefits.

Thus occupied I zoomed along the coast highway towards Malibu. I passed several inviting bars perched on the water front, but I didn't stop. I was headed now for Barnaby Flack's beach house; and Barnaby, I was sure, would have drinks to spare. Also, I hoped, a plot.

Plots were Barnaby's business. He was a movie and television script writer—the second best in the business, according to him. I'd met him when I'd been hired to act as adviser for the *Dirk Dagger—Soldier of Fortune* show, a series Barnaby had created.

A nice guy, Barnaby. It hadn't worried him a bit when he'd learned that I didn't know beans about soldier of fortuning.

"Neither do I," he'd confided, "and I dreamed up this show. But what the hell, a writer doesn't have to know what he's writing about. Did Dante have to go to hell before he could write *The Inferno*? How many science-fiction writers have been to the moon? All a writer needs to do is learn to fake convincingly. That, a formula to follow, and a complete set of the *National Geographic* will see him through anything."

He hadn't been kidding about the *National Geographic Magazine*. He really did have a complete set. As did most television writers who used exotic locales, he claimed.

"Greatest boon to adventure writers since the invention of the pencil, that magazine," he told me. "Like, I want to set one of Dirk's adventures in, say, Indonesia. What do I do? I turn to my trusty magazine file, that's what. Dig up some article with a title like *Through Storied Indonesia's Colorful Byways,* get out the old pencil and start jotting down phrases and place names and odd customs and stuff like that. Makes the script sound authentic as hell."

It did, too, oddly enough.

Barnaby had a lot of other writing short-cuts, too—like his plotting boards. The plotting board for the *Dirk Dagger* show, for example, consisted of a long bulletin board with various headings painted on the top, each heading representing a section of the complete formula that made up a half-hour *Dirk Dagger* television episode.

Like, *Shock Opening Scene; Dirk Meets Girl; Girl Menaced in Horrible Way by Villain; Clever Ruse by Which Dirk Rescues Girl*—and so on.

To match each of these headings or plot sections, Barnaby had a separate three-by-five card file with labels like *Ideas for Shock Openings; Horrible Ways to Menace a Girl; Clever Ruses,* etc.

This ingenious contraption made it possible for Barnaby to assemble complete plots out of spare parts in the same manner in which an automobile is put together on an assembly line—all he had to do was pull one card out of each filing cabinet and pin it under the right heading on the plotting board. And *voilà,* he had the complete skeleton of an original *Dirk Dagger* plot.

I must admit that the whole business had impressed me quite a bit. Before meeting Barnaby I'd always assumed that writing was something that required talent and imagination—but the way Barnaby did it, I could see that writing was really quite simple and easy. Almost child's play.

It wasn't even necessary to learn how to type—you could dictate into a tape recorder, as Barnaby did.

Still, easy though plotting might be, it wasn't my field, and I looked forward to dumping the problem of dreaming up an Adventure for Sam into Barnaby's hands.

## Chapter 8

BARNABY GREETED ME effusively and ushered me into his huge combination study and living room, a comfortable place with knotty pine walls and a picture window view of the Pacific.

"Good to see you again, Jake," he said, busying himself hauling two cans of beer out of a portable knotty-pine refrigerator and opening them. "What've you been up to?"

I took a long pull at my beer can and told him, in complete detail. Barnaby listened intently.

When I finished, he bounded to his feet and began to pace back and forth across his living room, head down, brows furrowed in thought, hands behind his back. Barnaby is a tall, greying guy with a Cyrano nose, and when he paced in that manner it gave him somewhat the appearance of a prematurely grey raven measuring its cage.

"Magnificent," he told me. "A magnificent concept. In bringing to life this kid Sam's daydreams we will not only be giving him a good time, we'll be pioneering new frontiers for hack—I mean commercial—writing. Just imagine what a great world this would be if we could all plot our own lives in advance, week by week, just like a TV serial. What adventures we could plot for ourselves! What conquests! What lavish seduction scenes, what feasts, what triumphs!"

"I don't think I'd like plotting my life like that," I told him. "I kind of like being surprised by what happens next. Most of the time anyway."

Barnaby ignored me. He was lost in a pacing reverie. "The very depths—I mean heights—of my writer's soul are stirred. If I plot a real-life adventure for this rich young punk, do you realize how utterly, how completely I will be able to satisfy my writing neuroses?"

"Huh?" I volunteered. "What neuroses?"

"All writers have neuroses," Barnaby told me. "That's why they become writers in the first place. And you know what a writer's basic neurosis is?"

I didn't, but I didn't bother replying. Barnaby would tell me anyway. He did.

"A writer's basic neurosis is the suppressed desire to play God, that's what. When I start a new story I gloat to myself. Why do I gloat? Because I have a whole bunch of human lives to play with. I can do anything, *anything* I like with my characters. You don't know what it's like, the feeling of power it gives me. In real life I go through a red light, some surly cop stops me and gives me a hard time. Plus a ticket."

"Yeah," I said, "but getting back to——"

"In real life," Barnaby continued relentlessly, "I meet

some gorgeous, shapely dame and make a pass at her. Like as not, she snubs me. Sneers at me. Spits at me."

"Yeah, spits," I said. "Getting back——"

"But things like that don't happen to me in my stories," Barnaby went on. "A traffic cop stops my hero—the traffic cop gets a fist in his belly. My hero meets a gorgeous dame—she climbs all over him. And vice versa."

"Yeah," I said, "climbs. Now getting back to——"

"It gives me an outlet for my frustrations and hostility," said Barnaby. "Like just yesterday some axe hole producer rejected one of my scripts. Did I sit and fume and get ulcers? I did not. I wrote the producer into a story I was working on—and then killed him dead." He rubbed his hands together gleefully. "Dropped him in boiling oil, that's what I did. Made me feel a hundred percent better."

"Yeah, oil," I said. "Now getting——"

"So you can see why I go for his setup you've outlined. Now I can manipulate real human beings—not just characters on paper or actors on a stage." His eyes gleamed happily. "Power, naked power will be mine."

"Yeah, power," I said. "Now——"

"Of course there are some precedents. People have had their lives written into real-life plots without their knowing it. Though not on such a lavish scale as you propose."

"They have?"

"Sure. Con men do it all the time. They want some mark to invest his money, they build a mock-up of a bank in some store front they've rented. Then they steer the mark into it, and the mark never even suspects that all the tellers and clerks and customers are really crooks playing a part.

"Then there's the badger game. The guy who busts into the hotel room isn't really married to the girl the sucker's been making love to—he and the girl are acting out parts, only the sucker doesn't know it.

"And sometimes con men stage a phony fight. Like, they invite some mark into a hotel room for a poker game. Then two of the con-men stage an argument, one pulls a gun and fires off a blank, the other bites down on a bladder full of chicken blood and falls to the floor with blood spurting out of his mouth. The mark thinks a real murder's been committed. Then a phony cop busts in and demands money for covering up the crime—and the mark pays without ever catching on that everybody was playing a part but him."

"Yeah," I agreed, "I guess there is a sort of parallel. You don't think the whole idea's too nutty, then?"

"Unconventional, perhaps; sublimely unconventional—but not nutty. Who thought up this wonderful scheme, anyhow? Not you, surely."

"A Dr. Bolingbrook, I think. He's Mr. Tamerlane's private psychologist."

Barnaby frowned. "A little guy with glasses and a head like a billiard ball? Real prissy and pompous?"

"That's him. You know him?"

Barnaby nodded again, thoughtfully. "I met him once, briefly—while I was doing research for *I, Con Man.*"

"He's a con man?"

"Not exactly. He's sort of an inspired quack. He's not a real psychologist, either—that doctorate of his came straight from a diploma mill in Kentucky."

I nodded wisely. I'd always figured Dr. Bolingbrook for a quack.

"Bolingbrook is to the psychology field," Barnaby continued, "what food faddists are to medicine. He's always coming up with some sort of psychological equivalent of Queen Bee Jelly or melon seeds. Still, I have to admit he's come up with an inspired idea for young Sam. If you can't get a guy to adjust to his environment, adjust the environment to the guy."

"It doesn't seem all that inspired to me," I objected. "So we set things up so that Sam can live like a swashbuckling soldier of fortune for a few weeks. How's that going to change him? We'll have to stop play acting eventually, and then Sam will be right back where he started: frustrated."

"Not," said Barnaby, "necessarily. He may get a lot of things out of his system. Also, if we plot his Adventure right, he'll have had a heady taste of success. And that can affect his whole future career, no matter what line of work he goes into eventually. You hear a lot of nonsense about what factors make one man successful and another a failure in life. If you ask me, the most important thing is luck—whether or not a guy succeeds in the first things he sets out to do.

"Once a guy succeeds a few times, he gets to thinking he's bound to succeed—sort of a built in will to win, a subconscious self-confidence. He's in the habit of winning, and like as not he'll go right on winning. Like those college rats."

"What rats?"

"An experiment they tried at one of the big universities. They took these two great big rats—real monsters—and threw 'em in the same cage so's they'd fight. Only before they did this, they slipped one rat a pep pill and the other one a tranquilizer. And which rat won?"

"The pep pill rat. Now getting back to——"

"Right, the pep pill rat. Over and over they let the two rats fight, and naturally the same rat always won. Then they stopped giving them pills—and *still* the first rat kept winning. Know what they did then? They started giving the winner rat transquilizers and the loser rat pep pills. And what happened?"

"The rats got sick."

"What happened was the first rat kept right on winning—he was in the *habit* of winning. Then they took two little tiny rats, real midgets, and did the same stunt with them. Know what they did then?"

"No," I said, "nor do I particularly care."

"What they did then was match the great big rat that had lost twenty fights in a row with the little teeny rat that had won twenty straight fights. And the little teeny rat won every time because he expected to win—just as the great big rat expected to lose."

"What does that prove?" I asked.

"It proves, Jake my boy, that success in life is a matter of conditioning."

"I always figured it was a matter of money."

"Money helps," Barnaby agreed. "And speaking of money, what's in this deal for me?"

"The satisfaction of pioneering new fields in hack writing," I told him. "And a chance to work off your neuroses."

Barnaby made a rude noise. "As the second best script writer in Hollywood I have been conditioned to getting big money."

"Two thousand a week?"

"Make it three."

"Sold," I said. "Now," I told him, "suppose I succeed—on my own initiative—in getting Walter C. Tamerlane to pay you *five* thousand a week. Will you kick back a grand to me?"

"You lousy, cheating crook!" screamed Barney. "I accept."

We shook hands on it. Things were looking up. Already I'd gotten myself a thousand dollar a week raise.

"Now," I said, "what about a plot for Sam's Adventure?"

"I'm glad you brought that up," said Barnaby. "I think that glubnon ixnag beldo obnorn."

To be absolutely truthful, I suppose that Barnaby didn't *really* say *glubnon ixnag beldo obnorn*—but that's what his words sounded like to me. And the reason they sounded like that was that a door to Barnaby's living room had just opened and a girl had slouched through—and I was too busy concentrating on the girl to bother listening to Barnaby.

The girl was small and blonde and busty and wearing a green belt around her waist.

Period.

## Chapter 9

FOR A LONG MOMENT I just sat frozen, staring at the little blonde. I was dimly aware that my mouth was hanging open a little, but I didn't give a hang.

Damn.

Hot damn.

HOT damn.

Hot DAMN.

Also wow.

The little blonde stuck one of her cute little thumbs into her cute little mouth and giggled. Then she took a few more mincing steps into the room, stopped, took her thumb out of her mouth, and cocked her head on one side while she examined me critically. Then she smiled, blinked her big blue (and to be truthful, somewhat vacuous) eyes at me, and giggled again.

I took that to mean that she didn't find me repulsive to look at. That made us even.

Like I said, she was a small girl; and now that she was a little closer I could see that she was a pretty young chick, too—but she wasn't what you'd call a child. Not physically.

She had what every girl would like to have and every guy wishes every girl had—only she had 'em in miniature. What I mean is, she looked like Jayne Mansfield as viewed through the wrong end of a telescope.

Her breasts, for example. If you measured them with a pair of outside micrometers I don't suppose they were much bigger than a pair of oversize tennis balls—which shape they closely resembled. But set on her diminutive rib cage they looked enormous.

Also sexy as hell. Also cute. Also pert. I don't know what you mean when you say a girl has cute, pert-looking breasts—but what I mean is that they sort of pout upwards.

Below her chest she was really small. Her waist looked tiny enough for me to circle with my fingers without my hands touching her at any point—though that would have been a pretty silly stunt to try.

Her hips were small, too—but only because she was as tiny as she was. Scaled up to normal size her hips would have been five axe handles across the beam.

But cuter, of course.

She giggled once again and stuck a thumb back into her mouth. The other thumb, this time.

"Sugar," said Barnaby mildly, "don't eat your thumb. You'll get——" He scratched his head. "Well, I don't know what you'll get. Just don't do it."

He turned to me. "She's always putting things in her mouth. You wouldn't believe some of the things she puts in her mouth. Isn't that right, Sugar?"

That got him a combination giggle and wriggle. With a naughty smile thrown in. A pleased, naughty smile. Evidently Sugar enjoyed putting into her mouth whatever it was she put in.

She turned back to me, giggled again, then turned and half glided, half wriggled out of the room. In case I haven't mentioned it, and I guess I haven't, she was wearing her blonde hair in a long braided pony tail that fell—believe it or not—to just below her buttocks. The pony tail bumped and switched back and forth across her little rump with each step she took. It was a nice rump. Every bit as pert and saucy as her breasts.

At the doorway she turned and peeked over her shoulder at me, giggled up a quick storm—and then was gone.

I turned and stared at Barnaby with blank surmise. "Who," I said, "the hell," I added, "was that?"

"That," said Barnaby, "was Sugar. She's sort of a house pet of mine. I found her."

"Found her?"

He nodded. "About two months ago I had this party here. Like a wild party you know? So along about dawn I got kind of bushed and passed out. When I woke up, there was Sugar, curled up at my feet like a lost puppy. All she had on was a belt. And since there wasn't any name on her belt I don't know who the hell her owner is."

"Didn't you ask her?"

"Sure. But all she did was stick her thumb in her mouth and giggle. Or maybe it was my thumb."

"Maybe she can't talk English," I suggested.

"I thought of that," said Barnaby. "I figured maybe she was some European starlet that had gotten mislaid. But she understands English all right. I've taught her to obey over a dozen simple commands. She *can* talk, too. Just the other day she said "Oh, spit!" That was just after she'd put something into her mouth that didn't agree with her. And from time to time she says "gimme!" Whenever she sees something she wants to put in her mouth she says that. That or she just sticks it in her mouth anyway."

I was about to tell Barnaby that I didn't believe a word of this outrageous story, when Sugar appeared in the doorway again. She was wearing a different belt—a bright red one this time—and nibbling on the end of a banana. She smiled at me over the end of her banana, giggled, then trotted over to sit on her haunches at my feet.

"She likes you," Barnaby said. "She's put on her best belt. I get her a new one every time I drive into town. She's got a whole closet full of 'em."

"Just—belts?"

Barnaby nodded. "She won't wear anything else. Got

some sort of complex about wearing clothes. Isn't that right Sugar?"

Sugar nodded: yes.

"Last month I tried to put a shirt on her," Barnaby continued. "Just for a change, you know. She didn't like it a bit."

Sugar shook her head: no.

"Started to whimper and cry. So I gave up. Last week I tried to put a pair of shorts on her—and she bit me."

Sugar giggled and chomped down hard on the last of her banana.

I took out my handkerchief and began to mop my brow. It wasn't a particularly hot afternoon, as California afternoons go, but my temperature was beginning to climb a bit anyway. Whenever a naked girl—with or without a belt—sits at my feet and smiles at me while she licks her lips my temperature is apt to climb a little.

And Sugar was no ordinary naked girl. Her skin was the color of golden browned toast and as smooth and flawless as a baby's. A shaft of sunlight slanting through Barnaby's picture window illumined her as if she were sitting under a golden spotlight, accenting the polished, glowing perfection of her flesh.

My temperature went up another notch.

Sugar swallowed the last of her banana, tossed the peel away, giggled, stuck her thumb in her mouth, and rolled over on her back, in which position she lay, knees and breasts jutting ceilingward, her head turned to one side the better to smile at me.

"She wants her tummy scratched," Barnaby explained. "She's just like a puppy in a lot of ways."

My temperature went up three notches at a bound. I closed my eyes and counted to ten. Slowly. Then, without opening my eyes, I said, "Barnaby, maybe *you* have gotten so damn blasé you can rub Sugar's tummy and let it go at that, but, but——"

"Sugar," said Barnaby sternly, "run out in the back yard and play. You're distracting Jake."

I kept my eyes closed until I heard a screen door bang, then opened them. Sugar was gone. But for the crumpled banana peel on the carpet—and the perspiration on my brow—it was hard to believe I hadn't just imagined her.

"Barnaby," I croaked, "I think one of us is nuts."

"Yeah," Barnaby agreed. "Sugar, I think. Either nuts or mentally deficient or both. She's cute, though. And housebroken. And *very* affectionate."

"Look," I said, "you can't keep a grown—or semi-grown—girl as a house pet."

"Why not?" asked Barnaby.

He had a point there. I guess.

"Now," said Barnaby, "to get back to Sam."

"Who? Oh, yeah. Sam."

Barnaby resumed his pacing. "Let me get this straight now. In five days' time you're going to get in touch with Sam. So we have to have an Adventure of some sort worked out by then. Right?"

"Right," I said.

"Okay. Now, the first thing we have to do is decide on the kind of plot we're going to involve Sam in. To some extent we're limited, you know."

"We are?"

"Sure. To be frank, I think Walter C. Tamerlane made a mistake in pulling you in on this. Now we'll have to cast Sam in the role of clean-cut young American side-kick. It would have been easier to cast him as a clean-cut young American accidentally involved in a web of intrigue."

"Don't," I said, "write me out of the script. I need the money."

Barnaby nodded, "It's too late now anyway. But it would have been a lot simpler with just Sam." He paced furiously. "The usual way of involving the hero in an adventure is to have some voluptuous but virginal girl in danger appeal to the hero for protection. Girl gets hero into danger, then hero gets into girl. And so on." He stabbed a finger in my direction. "You merely complicate matters."

"Never mind that," I said. "Just work out a plot."

Barnaby nodded. Silence reigned for a while as he paced back and forth, brow furrowed. "Under the circumstances," he said after a bit, "I think we'd be best off with a nice simple chase-type plot. With sex. And maybe some lost treasure tossed in."

"What do you mean 'chase'?" I asked. "You mean Sam and I do the chasing—or someone chases us?"

"Both. You and Sam—plus the Good Girl—will chase after some Lost or Mislaid Valuable Object. And the villains will chase after you and Sam. The beauty of this kind of plot is that it's flexible. We can make changes as we go along. Also it permits us to drag in a lot of exotic locales. Ditto exotic girls. I presume you want young Sam vamped by assorted exotic girls?"

I hadn't thought about that particular angle before. I thought about it. "Yeah," I said slowly, "I guess so."

"No guessing about it," said Barnaby. "If we're casting Sam as a clean-cut American soldier of fortune it's just about obligatory to have him vamped by exotic immoral girls."

Barnaby was right, of course. Still, the idea didn't exactly appeal to me. No matter how highly she was paid, it seemed kind of unfair to ask an erotic immoral girl to put out for a creep like young Sam.

A thought struck me. "Speaking of girls," I said, "what are we going to do about casting this epic?"

Barnaby frowned. "Hire actors, of course—unknown actors, prefarably. It would never do if Sam recognized some villain as someone he'd seen on TV the week before. His willing suspension of disbelief might start to buckle."

"I was thinking of the chicks we hire to make like exotic immoral girls."

"Ah," said Barnaby. "You have a point. It's one thing to hire a girl to play the part of a shameless trollop on TV. All she has to do is smile lasciviously and start to unzip her zipper. A slow fade or a lap-dissolve will protect her virtue. Obviously this will not serve in this case. The girls we hire will have to keep on unzipping. And then some. Still, it shouldn't present any real problem. Hollywood is full of call girls with acting experience—not to mention actresses who double as party girls." He stopped abruptly in mid-stride and clapped a hand to his forehead. "*Party Girl!* My God, I was supposed to be at a script conference ten minutes ago."

He turned and dashed for the door.

"Hey wait!" I yelled.

"Sorry," Barnaby called over his shoulder, "I gotta talk to a producer about this movie called *I, Party Girl* that I'm scripting." He grabbed his hat. "Stick around if you like. I'll be back in a few hours." Then the door banged behind him and he was gone.

"Crazy," I said aloud. "Everyone I meet these days is crazy."

Across the room somebody giggled as if to confirm my statement. I looked up. Sugar, thumb in mouth, was standing in a doorway smiling at me.

Then she pulled her thumb from her mouth and, slowly and deliberately, began to unbuckle her belt.

## Chapter 10

When she got the belt buckle unfastened she held the two ends of her belt together for a couple of seconds, then let it drop to the floor. Sugar wasn't ninety-nine and fourty-four one-hundreths percent nude any more. She was a hundred percent nude.

Somehow it made a difference.

Sugar giggled again, tucked her left thumb into her mouth, then turned and began to stroll provocatively away. After a few paces she peeked over her shoulder to see if I was following.

I was.

I followed her saucy, swaying little buttocks through a species of sun porch then on out into Barnaby's back garden. A big beach mattress was spread on the lawn. Sugar spread herself on the mattress and smiled at me.

Hog dog. Sex in the sun. I hadn't sexed it up outdoors in a long time. I tore off my sports jacket.

Already the hot blooded little blonde animal lying nakedly before me was reaching up hungry arms towards me. No.

Only one arm. Holding a bottle of sun tan oil.

Hell and damnation. Did she just want me to oil her up for a sun bath? Apparently. I sighed and took the bottle of sun tan oil from her. After all, I had nothing else to do right them.

Sugar smiled happily and rolled over on her tummy while I knelt beside her, slopped oil on my hands, and began to rub it into her back.

Her flesh was deliciously warm beneath my sliding fingers, and her Southern exposure presented a pleasing spectrum of tactile response—sleek, firm flesh over the subtle compound curve of her backbone and the flight deck of her shoulder blades; plumply resilient flesh along the oil-soaked curves of her thighs and the quivering globes of her buttocks.

Beneath my sliding, cupping, squeezing hands Sugar began to squirm with sensual pleasure. Sugar might not be bright, but she knew what she liked. So did I.

I dug my fingers hard into the rounded hills of her rump, kneading the oil-slippery hot flesh, feeling it ripple and squirm and shiver beneath my grasp.

What, I thought, a happy invention girl flesh is: a joy to encounter under any circumstances and all conditions. Wet girl flesh, for example. How soul satisfying it is to swim naked at night with a naked female companion, and then touch bodies in the shallows, feeling slippery wet flesh as cool as marble thrust against you.

How erotically delightful to toy with soft dry flesh on a soft dry bed; how exciting to fondle hot, sweat-soaked female skin when the passion of your mutual love-making has brought temperatures to the boiling point.

What other substance—save girl flesh—has so many textures and temperatures and degrees of resiliency? And every one as erotic as hell.

I cupped my palms over Sugar's saucy buttocks and shook them hard. They shivered and bounced happily. Sugar purred contentedly for a few moments; then, with a funny sound somewhere between a giggle and a murmur of ecstasy, she flipped herself over.

I began to feel up—I mean oil—her front side. All the way up her front side my oiled hands slid, and all the way down. Over the golden columns of her thighs, the insolently flaring sweep of her hips, the tiny upturned golden bowl of her belly. Sugar's tummy was not flat—which suited me just fine. It may be fashionable and chic for a girl's stomach to be absolutely flat, but (to my way of thinking) it isn't natural. Or sexy.

Don't get me wrong. I don't mean I dig fat tummies on girls; not at all; it's just that I don't like girls to be flat—anywhere.

I let my oily fingers slide teasingly around and over

Sugar's tummy for a while, then moved up to oil the succulently saucy globes of her breasts.

Then a tremor seemed to run through her whole body and abruptly she sat up. And reached for me.

No.

She was only reaching for the bottle of sun tan oil. I gave it to her. She poured a pool of oil into the upturned palm of her other hand and then looked at me inquiringly.

"You bet," I said, and began tearing off my clothes. What the hell. I could use a little tan. And if Sugar wanted to have a little fun oiling me, who was I to deny a dumb, beautiful, no doubt passionate blonde her kicks?

So I stripped in record time and stretched out on my back in the warm sun. Sugar began to oil me.

I closed my eyes and tried to relax while Sugar's slender fingers began to massage my body with oil. All my body. All parts and sections of my body. Over parts of my body I'd forgotten I owned Sugar's stroking, fondling fingers moved. And squeezed and teased and clasped.

Damn. Hot *flaming* damn.

Relax? Who was I trying to kid? I wasn't relaxed a bit; to the contrary, my whole body was getting rigid with excitement.

I opened my eyes. Sugar was kneeling astride me, a blissful if somewhat stupid smile on her face as she ran her oily fingers over my chest. Her breasts swayed gently in tempo with her moving hands. I reached up and cupped them lightly. That got me a broader smile and she wriggled her chest a little so that her breasts seemed to squirm in my grasp.

Soon Sugar forgot to massage my chest and began making nasal murmuring sounds of pleasure. I kept on gently squeezing her breasts, but now I was pushing a little too, pushing her back gently until she wasn't so much kneeling over me as sitting on me.

Sugar giggled. Evidently an idea had come to her. It had. She raised her plump little rump a few inches and then settled herself on me again in a more comfortable position. A much more comfortable position. For both of us.

Yes.

Most certainly.

Absolutely.

With bells on.

Once upon a time I remember seeing an old medieval print called the zones of man or something stupid like that. Anyhow, what it was was a drawing of a man wearing just a fig leaf, with these concentric circles drawn over him, moving out from the fig leaf like ripples. Indicating something or other.

But that was how I felt right then, lying there under the blazing sun and the churning Sugar—like ripples of liquid fire were spreading out through my entire body, spreading out from a metaphorical fig leaf. Only I wasn't wearing a fig leaf of course. I was wearing Sugar instead.

Faster and faster moved the ripples of pleasure fire, faster and faster and hotter and hotter until the ripples became an artesian well of flame and Sugar seemed to catch fire as well and I heard her whimper and felt her body move like a runaway cement mixer.

My clawing fingers closed over the softness of her hips and I pulled her tight, tight to me as my body arched shuddering up off the mattress, and dimly, as from a long way away, I heard Sugar screech as if she'd become impaled upon a spear of fire. And then it was over, and the agonizing moment of ultimate truth was gone.

Gone but not forgotten, you might say.

## Chapter 11

WITH ITS JETS throttled back to a whisper the airliner dropped in a long glide through high banks of fleecy clouds until we emerged again suddenly into brilliant sunshine. And there, directly beneath us, lay the island of Trinidad—glittering, green and vast in a sapphire sea. It looked real pretty, I must say.

I pointed out the window for Sam's benefit. "That's Port of Spain directly below. We'll be landing at Piarco airport, over there to the right."

Sam peered through the window. "That's Piarco airport?"

I nodded wisely.

Sam shook his head dubiously. "Looks more like the city dump to me."

I smiled wisely.

*"We are now heading in for a landing,"* crackled the pilot's voice over the loudspeaker. *"Piarco airport is five miles ahead. Below to the right you can now see the city dump. One of the finest in the West Indies."*

Sam smiled faintly.

"Uh, yes," I said. "I guess that is the dump. They've, uh, changed things quite a bit since I was adventuring here last."

Needless to say I'd never been to Trinidad before in my life. And if you're wondering what Sam and I were doing arriving there via jet, I have to confess that right then I was wondering myself.

So, more than likely, was Barnaby—the louse.

After sexing it up in the sun with Barnaby's house pet, Sugar, I'd hastily and guiltily washed the sun tan oil off me in Barnaby's swimming pool, put on my clothes, and settled back to await his return.

Eight cans of beer and four hours later I was still waiting. I was also feeling a lot less guilty about jumping Sugar. What the hell, if Barnaby was so rude as to leave his guests standing around waiting for him for hours on end, what else did he expect them to do except jump Sugar? Especially as Sugar was so eminently jumpable.

So I jumped on Sugar again—to our mutual satisfaction.

I drank more beer. I fumed more hours. Only I didn't fume quite so much now, because now I'd devised a system for reducing my nervous tension—said system consisting of jumping Sugar on the hour every hour.

On the half hour she jumped me.

A real little female, Sugar.

And so it went. For five days and nights it went like that—with time out only for sleeping, drinking, splashing in Barnaby's swimming pool and raiding his well-stocked refrigerators. (He had six on hand—evidently to keep him and Sugar supplied in the event of nuclear war.)

From time to time I lost my temper and stalked up and down swearing and cursing and wondering where the hell Barnaby had gotten to. I also ran up his phone bill by periodically calling around to various bistros in an attempt to scare him up—with no success.

But most of the time I just lolled around the beach house sunning, swimming, drinking, eating—and playing with Sugar. If you're wondering why I didn't just drive home I'll tell you: I kept figuring that as long as I'd waited as long as I had, I might as well wait a bit more. After all, Barnaby had to return sometime.

Also I was having a ball with Sugar.

All kinds of balls. Sugar was certainly a playful little animal—and quite imaginative when it came to devising new games to play.

Like, sometimes we played Follow the Leader. It was a very simple game. Sugar always led and I always followed. We played it like this. First Sugar would get on all fours and begin to crawl away from me, giggling and looking over her shoulder as she went. Then I got on all fours and followed.

It always ended the same way, too. Sugar would crawl coquettishly a few feet and then stop—no doubt to catch her breath. And, inevitably, I would have been crawling so fast I couldn't stop in time to prevent colliding with her.

Since I was always crawling directly astern of her this always meant that my chin and chest slid right up over her plump little rump and kept on sliding until my chin was resting on the nape of her neck.

Sugar never seemed to mind my bumping into her that way. To the contrary, she always giggled and started wagging her little tail, metaphorically speaking. It was a reaction that never failed to stir me.

We played other games, too. Sometimes we played Octopus. Sugar was always the octopus and I was always the victim—the object of the game being for Sugar to wrap her hot little tentacles around me—and squeeze. She was good at squeezing, was Sugar.

Sometimes, too, we played Wolves and Tigers—a game in which we flung ourselves at each other like wild beasts, pretending we were going to devour each other. Being devoured by Sugar was quite an experience, believe me.

And once we found a couple of Aqualungs and slid into Barnaby's pool, there to slide into a close embrace eight feet under water. That was when I learned that not only can it be done, but it's a hell of a lot of fun doing it that way. Different, though.

Making love underwater isn't a matter of violent physical motion—rather, it's an art that calls for a sort of sensuous merger; a pulsing, skin sliding, writhing blending of bodies. Helped along by Sugar's imaginative control of her squeezing muscles. (What arms Sugar had! What legs!)

Then, too, there's an unreal, dreamlike quality about making love under water; with your eyes half closed and no sense of gravity you don't know which end is up—and that's half the fun. You sort of tumble gently end over end, floating in crystal green space. Pulsing as you float.

So what with one thing and another the five days passed not unpleasantly.

Still I was glad when, five days to the hour after he'd left, Barnaby returned. Glad but mad. I would have been even madder save for the fact that poor Barnaby looked as if he'd had all the punishment he could take. His face alone presented an interesting color combination: pasty white skin, blue circles around each eye, and spectacular red eye balls.

"Where," I snarled, "the hell have you been?"

"Out," said Barnaby. "Out cold part of the time, but mostly out living it up. After the conference we had a few drinks, and that led to a party, and that led to a wild party which turned into an orgy. And you know how formal Hollywood orgies are—you just can't break away early. It isn't done." He groaned and put his hands to his head.

"I don't mean to seem rude old man," he told me, "but would you mind just—going away? I've gotta get some sleep."

"Like hell I'll go away!" I yelled. "What about the plot—for Sam and me?"

Barnaby cringed. "Don't shout so, please. I think I'm missing part of my head. What plot? Oh. Oh yes. Forgotten about that." He laughed feebly.

"Forgotten?" I yelled. "Don't you realize you're drawing five grand a week—less a grand kickback to me—just to serve as my private writer? Don't you realize that I'm supposed to call Sam before midnight and tell him the

Royal Road to Romance lies open? That—that—that——"

"Stop spluttering so loud," pleaded Barnaby, rubbing his blood shot eyes. "Can't you see I'm near death?"

He did look sort of sick, I had to admit. Lucky dog. It must have been some orgy to leave him in shape like that.

Sugar came trotting up solicitously carrying an open beer can. Barnaby gulped down half of it groaning, then poured the rest over his brow. "What," he demanded of nobody in particular, "did I do to deserve this?"

"I don't know," I snarled. "What did you do?"

Barnaby opened one eye and leered at me. "Everything. What a ball I had." Then he closed his eye again and groaned.

"What about a plot?" I repeated.

"Plot. Yes. Don't worry, Jake. I'll work something out. Soon. Recently. Not right now though. Have to get some shut-eye first. Anyhow, you don't need a plot just right yet. You and Sam can start adventuring without one."

He lurched unsteadily across his living room, his right index finger extended. "Map on the wall here someplace," he muttered. Five or six lurches brought him and his index finger to a map of the world pinned to the wall.

"What's my finger pointing to?" he inquired. "I'm not focusing so good right now."

I peered at the map. "The Gobi Desert."

"Out of bounds," muttered Barnaby. He stabbed again with his finger. "Now what?"

"Trinidad," I told him.

"Fine, fine. You and Sam go to Trinidad. Fine place, Trinidad. Exotic and all that. Melting pot of the Spanish Main. Singapore of the Caribbean."

"And what do we do when we get there?" I inquired suspiciously.

"By the time you get there," Barnaby assured me, "I'll have figured something out."

"That's just plain silly," I said. "We can't just go off blindly to some place for no reason."

"Why not?" demanded Barnaby. "I told you a chase plot would be best. Besides, Sam won't know you don't have any reason for going there. It'll all be exotic adventure to him."

"Maybe," I said dubiously. "What reason do I give him for us zooming off to the West Indies, though? He's bound to ask."

Barnaby nodded—and instantly clutched his aching head again, wincing. "Tell him—tell him the Armenian is going to meet you there."

"The Armenian?"

"Right. Half the adventure stories I write start with a mysterious Armenian arranging to meet the hero in some faraway place. I don't always call him an Armenian, of course—sometimes he's The Fat Man, or The Levantine, or The Polish Colonel. Just so he's an Exotic Foreign Man of Mystery. In working out my plots, however, I think of him as the Armenian."

"You mean you use the same characters over and over?"

"Of course. With a different name who knows the difference? Especially on television."

If all this sounds kind of absurd to you, I can assure you it struck me exactly the same way. On the other hand, what else could I do but play along? There wasn't time to hire another writer.

So after arguing a bit more with Barnaby, I dialed Tamerlane Castle and asked to speak to Sam.

"Sam," I said when he came to the phone, "this is Jake. I'm onto something big. Real big. You still want to throw in your luck with me—even if our quest leads us into terrible danger?"

"You bet," said Sam. "What kind of quest?"

I glared at Barnaby. "I'm not sure yet, Sam. But the Armenian's mixed up in it. And if he's mixed up in it, it has to be big. Uh, real big."

"The Armenian? Who's he? Doesn't he have a name?"

I nudged Barnaby who was listening drowsily on an extension. "What's the Armenian's name?" I hissed, covering the phone mouthpiece.

Barnaby frowned. "Just say he has a hundred names and a hundred faces, but to those who prowl the international underworld he's known simply as 'the Armenian'."

I repeated this gem of prose to Sam. It silenced him if nothing else.

"The Armenian wants us to meet him in Port of Spain," I added.

"Port of Spain, the capital city of Trinidad, population 740,000, average mean temperature 76 degrees?" inquired Sam.

"That's the place," I said, reflecting that Sam really had boned up on exotic places. "Meet me at the airport in an hour. We'll take the seven o'clock plane to Miami."

"Okay," said Sam. "What kind of side-arms shall I bring?"

"Uh, better not bring any guns," I advised him. "We might have trouble getting them through customs."

"Knives?"

"No knives either." Sam was sure a lethal-minded young man. To placate him I added, "We can always pick up some artillery on the spot if we need to."

"Good," said Sam. "See you at the airport." He hung up. Somehow it seemed to me it would have been a little more seemly for him to have waited for me to hang up—but what the hell. Kids just don't have any respect for their elders these days.

"See," said Barnaby, yawning and stretching out on his couch, "I told you everything was simple." He yawned again and held up one foot so that Sugar could unlace his shoe. "Have a good trip."

"Wait!" I said. "Don't fall asleep yet. What do I do when we get there?"

"Mark time enigmatically," mumbled Barnaby, "then slip away from Sam and call me. I'll have something plotted for you by then." And with that he began to snore gently.

Which left me with nothing to do but pat Sugar a fond farewell and dash for the airport.

Sam was waiting for me, looking even more pimply faced and adolescent than I'd remembered. "I've already bought my ticket," he announced. "I think it best if we each pay our own way—and then split whatever profits we make fifty-fifty."

"Uh, sure," I said. Privately, however, it struck me as being somewhat presumptious of young Sam to cut himself in for fifty percent. After all, *I* was the experienced soldier of fortune, so far as Sam knew, and Sam the mere apprentice.

However, since there weren't going to be any profits, I could afford to be generous about splitting them.

With that thought, I bought my ticket and we boarded the plane. If Sam was thrilled to the depths of his adolescent soul at the idea of departing on his first Adventure he managed not to show it—he fell asleep almost as soon as the plane was airborne.

I spent most of the flight pouring over travel folders I'd picked up at the airport. Sam had somehow gotten the impression that I was an old Trinidad hand, and it seemed a shame to disillusion him.

At Miami, after booking seats on the morning plane, we checked in at a hotel. While Sam was showering I made a couple of futile attempts to call Barnaby. The operator explained that someone was answering his phone all right—but all they did was giggle.

Hence it was that when, next morning, our plane landed at Port of Spain I hadn't the least notion of what was in store for us. Which may have been just as well.

## Chapter 12

AFTER CLEARING through the airport customs I hired a taxi—painted shocking pink—and had the driver take us on an abbreviated tour of the city.

I had to admit that Barnaby had picked an exotic enough town for the first stage of our—as yet unwritten—adventure. Port of Spain, the travel pamphlets had claimed, is a bubbling melting pot of Chinese, Moslems, Hindus, Englishmen, Portuguese, Syrians, Spaniards, Sikhs, Parsees and assorted South Americans. And, after our taxi had threaded its way through half a dozen winding, torturous, narrow streets, I began to believe them.

Pukka sahibs with swagger sticks and monocles mingled with Hindu holy men, slit-skirted Chinese girls, turbaned Sikhs and sport-shirted tourists. Colorful. Sort of like a travelogue come to life.

"We are now," I informed Sam, "driving through the heart of Port of Spain, the Singapore of the Western Hemisphere, a polyglot cosmopolitan metropolis that is also the native habitat of the calypso and the steel band."

Sam stared at me coldly. "You sound like a tourist

pamphlet," he said. "What hotel are we going to stop at?"

As he spoke, the taxi started to crawl, honking past a faded sign that read *The Potted Palm Hotel—Cheap Rooms*. "This one," I said on impulse, and told the driver to stop.

"Looks like a dump to me," complained Sam as we piled out.

And so it did, for a fact. On the other hand, it looked —to me at least—more mysterious and Eric Ambler-ish than the fancy concrete and chrome luxury hotels we'd passed earlier. And if Sam hankered for atmosphere it was up to me to see that he got it.

The lobby of the *Potted Palm* looked even more promising as a setting for intrigue—battered bamboo chairs and bedraggled palms (potted) scattered haphazardly about; framed pictures of Queen Victoria and Prince Albert on the wall; and, behind what passed for the reception desk, an enigmatic looking Chinese clerk.

The clerk disenigmatized himself long enough to show me to a pair of dingy adjoining rooms. He also sold me a bottle of 150-proof Demarara rum. I sat on the edge of my bed and took a long pull from the bottle. There were several glasses handy, but I felt that drinking from the bottle was more in keeping with my dashing soldier-of-fortune character.

Sam sat himself down primly on a hard chair and declined helping himself to a swig.

"I don't drink," he said. "Long ago I decided never to sap my strength by ingesting alcohol."

I pulled out a pack of cigarettes and raised my eyebrows questioningly.

"Smoking saps one's strength, too," Sam said.

I took another swig from my bottle, lit a cigarette, and inquired: "What are you saving your strength for, sex?"

"Sex," said Sam, "also has a tendency to sap one's strength."

I stared at him. Then I took another, king-size swig from the rum bottle. All of a sudden I felt I needed it. "Sam," I said when I'd quit choking, "may I ask you a personal question?"

"Certainly," said Sam.

"It's just this. If you don't approve of smoking, or

drinking, or sexing it up—then why in hell do you want to become a soldier of fortune?"

"I do not follow the logic of your question," said Sam.

I took another quick swig. "Sam," I said, "don't you realize that it—it's traditional for soldiers of fortune to smoke, drink and live it up? It's, well, part of the game."

Sam blinked at me sternly. "Do you consider your profession a mere game?"

I considered. "Yes," I said, "if you put it that way. You know, like it's not whether you win or lose and all that, but how you play."

Sam shook his head severely. "I do not agree. I have made a close scientific study of the lives of dozens of soldiers of fortune, both fictional and authentic, and I have reached the conclusion that a tendency towards dissipation is the major occupational disease of such men. I intend to avoid making a similar error."

I took another swig from my bottle.

"As to why I have selected this particular profession as my future career, the reason is simply that I have always been fascinated by the scientific application of violence to human affairs."

Port of Spain is a tropical city, and it was a hell of a hot afternoon that afternoon. Nevertheless I felt suddenly chilled. Sam *was* a loony. Even though I didn't dig the violent life myself, I could at least have understood a teen-age boy who daydreamed about becoming a soldier of fortune for kicks. But to want to become one simply in order to apply violence scientifically . . .

"You are shivering," observed Sam. "Perhaps you have caught some dread tropical fever. There are a number of dread tropical fevers rampant in this part of the world, for example——"

"Never mind," I snapped. "Tell me, Sam, doesn't all this—this exotic atmosphere and all that *do* anything to you—doesn't it excite you?"

"Not particularly," said Sam. He pondered. "It interests me, however."

Well that was something, anyhow. At least his old man's money wasn't being completely wasted. And perhaps, I reflected, taking another swig of rum, perhaps Sam was more human than he seemed. Perhaps all his talk about cold, logical violence was just a big front.

The mere fact that he so obviously couldn't distinguish fact from fiction was encouraging. It meant he was still young and unsure of things.

Either that or he was completely crazy.

"Now," said Sam, "*I* have some questions. You say that while you were in Los Angeles a person known to you as the Armenian contacted you and asked you to meet him here in Port of Spain?"

I nodded.

"And he contacted you how?"

"Why, uh, he wrote me a letter—which I naturally chewed up and swallowed after I'd read it."

"But," objected Sam, "on the plane it seems to me you told me he telephoned you."

"Uh, so he did." I admitted. "First he wrote me and then he phoned to make sure I'd gotten the message."

"I see," said Sam. "This gives us a clue as to his personality. He must be a methodical person who believes in leaving nothing to chance."

"That's him," I said.

"And you don't know his real name?"

I shook my head. "He has a hundred names, but to the international underworld he is known only as the Armenian."

"So you told me," agreed Sam. "What sort of a person is he, anyway?"

I thought about this. Actually I didn't have to think too hard—I'd already begun to form a sort of mental picture of our mythical employer: a vague, shapeless, sinister man of great wealth who kept himself behind the scenes.

"He's a vague, shapeless, sinister man of great wealth," I told Sam, "who keeps himself behind the scenes."

Sam swallowed this bit of nonsense without blinking. "I see. And you have no idea why he wishes to hire you—us, that is?"

"You can say that again," I agreed.

"But," continued Sam, "considering your reputation, it must doubtless be for some mission that is illegal, dangerous, violent, or all three."

"You bet," I agreed. "They don't come any more illegal, dangerous or violent than Jake of Arabia."

Sam said nothing. Somehow his silence bugged me.

When we'd first met, his attitude toward me had been close to hero worship. Then he'd been respectful. Now he was barely polite. I had a nasty feeling that Sam didn't consider me a particularly efficient soldier of fortune.

Also, Sam was entirely too calm to suit me. Hell, I was getting more of a kick out of our adventure than he was—and I knew it was a wild goose chase.

I decided to inject a note of subtle menace into the proceedings. I tiptoed over to the window and peered out cautiously, as if expecting a hail of bullets to greet my appearance.

"Looking for the Armenian?" inquired Sam. "By the way, how will the Armenian know where to reach us?"

"He has his ways," I said cryptically. "But it's not the Armenian I'm worried about; it's the, uh, Bulgarian."

At last I had startled Sam. At any rate, he blinked. "The Bulgarian? Who's he?"

A good question. "Why, uh, the Bulgarian is another vague, sinister man of great wealth who keeps behind the scenes. He's also the sworn enemy of the Armenian."

"This is most interesting," said Sam, producing a small black book. "I must make a note."

"You fool!" I yelled. "Never put anything on paper. Don't you know even the elementary rules of soldier of fortuning?"

"You're right, of course," said Sam. "I didn't think. Thank you for reprimanding me."

"Any time, old man." I clapped him on the shoulder in a friendly but condescending manner. "In this game, Sam, you've got to keep your wits about you twenty-four hours a day. Come on, let's go out and reconnoiter."

"Reconnoiter what?"

"I'll know that," I said, "after we've reconnoitered." I led the way downstairs. In the lobby a small, sallow-faced man wearing a shabby white suit and a red fez sat in one of the bamboo easy chairs reading a newspaper. He stared at us sharply as we clumped into the lobby. Then he folded his newspaper and strolled slowly out the hotel entrance to the street.

He looked, it struck me, fortuitously sinister. I stopped dead and nudged Sam with my elbow. "I could be wrong," I muttered out of the side of my mouth, "but I've a feeling that bird in the red fez is up to no good."

"I was thinking the same thing," muttered Sam.

It was an effort to keep from smiling. Sam sure was intrigue-happy—even seeing menace in a harmless little man in a red——

"Pssst!" said someone. I jumped barely six inches.

The Chinese room clerk beckoned us to his desk with a crooked finger, a gesture that made him look pleasingly furtive. "You are," he whispered when Sam and I had approached to whispering distance, "perhaps hot? The police perhaps look for you?"

"Certainly not," I snapped. "We're respectable—that is—why do you ask?"

"The little man in the red fez, the one who just left. He was asking many questions about you."

"Well I'll be damned," I said. "What do you think of that, Sam. Sam?"

Sam was gone. Not completely gone. I caught a glimpse of him sprinting out the hotel entrance. I sprinted in pursuit. Suddenly I was tackled around the ankles. No, I'd just tripped over a bamboo footstool. I picked myself up and dashed on.

Outside the hotel the narrow street was almost dark and totally empty. No sign of Sam. No sign of anybody. Nothing but a faint gurgling sound. Gurgling sound? I took a few quick steps in the direction the noise seemed to be coming from. Just past the hotel was a small, dark alley. And lying on his back in the alley was the little man in the red fez—making gurgling sounds. Considering that Sam was sitting on his chest busily choking him I could hardly blame him.

"Sam!" I yelled. "Quit that!"

"Just trying to get the truth out of this swine," explained Sam, choking the little man even harder. "Caught him skulking in the alley waiting for us to come out—gave me some wild spur-of-the-moment story about being a method actor named Smith playing a practical joke on us. But I'll choke the real truth out of him. He's obviously one of the Bulgarian's men." He shook the little man angrily. The little man said nothing but gurgled plaintively.

What to do? If I told Sam the little man had most likely been speaking the truth, our adventure—and my salary—would come screeching to a halt. On the other hand, I could hardly stand idly by while Sam choked him. I'd have Actor's Equity on my neck.

"Sam," I said with sudden inspiration, "this guy may be just a decoy to draw us away from the hotel—so the Bulgarian can search our rooms!"

"Say, that's right," agreed Sam, loosening his grip on the little man's throat a bit.

"Better dash back to the hotel," I advised, "and see if you can catch the Bulgarian red-handed. I'll stay here and continue choking the truth out of this act—uh, swine. Hurry! Don't let them steal the map, whatever happens!"

"Right!" barked Sam, and dashed back towards the *Potted Palm.*

I helped the little man to his feet, dusted him off and handed him his fez.

"You," I said, "are in Barnaby's employ, I presume?"

"*Was,* you mean," snarled the little man, fingering his bruised throat. "What's with that guy?" He jerked his head in the direction Sam had dashed in. "He *crazy* or something?"

"In a word, yes," I admitted.

"Just wait until the union hears about this," muttered the little man. "I'm relaxing on the set in Kingston—that's in Jamaica, you know?—where we shooting this TV series *I, Pirate,* you know?"

"I know," I said. "I mean—I didn't know."

"And my old friend Barnaby calls. Do me a favor, he says, and make yourself a fast five hundred bucks. Hop a plane to Port of Spain, he says, buy yourself a red fez, hunt up two guys named Tamerlane and O'Day, and then hang around for a few hours looking furtive. Like it's a joke? Some joke." He rubbed his throat again.

"Yeah," I said. "Well, that's show business. Uh, better make tracks before Sam gets back. He's kind of a bloodthirsty kid—as you may have guessed."

"You ain't kidding," said the little red-fezzed man, and started making tracks.

I stooped, rubbed my hands on the ground, smeared dust on my face and clothes. Then I waited for Sam to dash back. Back he dashed in record time. "No one in our rooms," he said. "I don't know what—where'd he go? That swine I was choking?"

"He got away from me," I gasped. "Four of his friends jumped me from behind. I fought and fought but—" I shrugged. "That's show bus—I mean, that's the way the ball bounces."

"Huh," said Sam. "Only four, and you let them take you?"

"I suppose you could have done better?" I asked icily.

Sam pursed his thin lips. "Frankly, I do." He frowned. "And come to think of it—why did you send me dashing back to the hotel to keep the Bulgarian from stealing our map? We don't *have* any map."

I snapped my fingers. "That's right, Sam. This caper doesn't have a map. I've been on so many different capers lately I sometimes get a little confused."

"So," said Sam coldly, "I've noticed. Well, what now?"

What? I stuck a cigarette in my mouth, lit it, inhaled, then closed my eyes for a moment to think.

"Phhhht!" said Sam, and jerked the cigarette out of my mouth.

I opened my eyes and glared at him. "God damn it, Sam, if you want a cigarette ask for one—don't pull it out of my mouth while making contemptuous noises."

Sam stared at me. "I didn't. I don't smoke. Maybe somebody shot it out of your mouth using a gun with a silencer attachment."

"Don't be juvenile," I snarled, and stuck another cigarette in my mouth.

*Phhhhht!* went a gun with a silencer—and away went my second cigarette.

"Hit the dirt!" I yelled. Sam joined me quickly. Prone on our stomachs in the alley we stared into the surrounding darkness in panic and detached interest. That is, I stared with panic and Sam—as he told me later—stared with detached interest. The cold-blooded jerk.

*Phhhhht*—SMACK!

"That one went over our heads," Sam whispered. "Hit the brick wall behind us."

*Phhhhht*—SPANG!

"That one must have hit a garbage can. He's shooting wild now."

"Yeah, wild," I muttered. "Where is he? Or them?"

"Just one guy, I think," whispered Sam. "Over behind

those trees. Let's encircle him. You attract his fire while I circle back through the alley and get behind him."

"Suppose *you* attract his fire," I suggested, "and *I'll* back out the alley."

Sam nodded agreement and I began wriggling my way backwards squid fashion.

*Phhhhht*—SPANG! went the silenced gun. Another garbage can.

*Phhhhht*—THUNK! Bullet must have hit something wooden. A tree perhaps. Or Sam's head.

I wriggled backwards faster, negotiated a sharp turn—and found myself in the adjoining street. I scrambled to my feet. "Courage, Sam!" I yelled. "I'm on my way!"

And so I was—on my way out of danger as fast as I could run.

## Chapter 13

I RAN WITH A SPEED negligibly slower than sound for the first couple of blocks, then slowed to a panic stricken dash and finally, after I reached a more brightly lit section, reduced speed to a nervous lope.

Pretty soon I came to a massive building which a sign proclaimed was the Queen's Park Hotel. The pamphlets, I recalled, stressed that the Queen's Park was to Trinidad what Shepheard's Hotel was to Cairo and Raffles to Singapore. Good. It ought to have a telephone. It did.

Thanks to the marvels of modern-day electronics I almost immediately had the pleasure of waking Barnaby from a sound sleep.

"God damn it, Jake!" he roared. "Have you any idea what time in the morning it is out here? Have you no consideration?" His voice faded. "No, Sugar—don't put that in your mouth right now. Sugar," he explained for my benefit, "loves to eat apples in bed."

"So did Eve," I said. "To hell with Sugar. What I want to know is——"

"Don't shout!" yelled Barnaby. "Has Ed Smith started lurking yet?"

"A little guy in a red fez? Yeah, he's been lurking. It

almost proved fatal, too. And speaking of fatal tricks, did you or did you not hire somebody to shoot at us?"

"You bet," said Barnaby. "Guy named Enrico the Great. He's an old friend of mine—does a fancy shooting act with circuses. I located him in Sarasota and told him to hop a plane down and jolly things up for you boys."

"Oh," I said. I felt momentarily less upset—at least the shooting hadn't been for real. Then I got upset again. Like hell it hadn't been for real. "You bastard!" I yelled. "Do you realize I might have been killed—not to mention Sam. How good a shot is this Enrico character?"

"Ninety-nine percent accurate," said Barnaby. "I met him when I was writing a circus movie. Got to be very good friends with him and his wife—late wife, poor girl."

"*Late* wife?"

"Yeah. Tragic bit. An unintended switch on the William Tell gimmick. Enrico goofed and shot her head out from under an apple."

I swallowed hard. "You're kidding?"

Barnaby snickered evilly. "Yeah, I'm kidding." He lowered his voice. "She wasn't really his wife, you see—just some empty-headed girl he picked up. And——"

"Don't wisecrack long distance," I snarled. "Who or what else can I expect to come crawling in the hotel window tonight?"

"Well, I tried to reach another old friend of mine, Sticker Sid, a professional knife thrower. I figured a few knives flung past Sam's head would liven things up nicely. A real sharp guy, Sid—quite a cut up, too; a gay blade you might say. But I couldn't locate him."

"Good. Don't. By the way, I've introduced a new mythical character into this adventure—the Bulgarian. He's supposed to be the sworn enemy of the Armenian."

"Tsk, tsk," said Barnaby. "That's pretty corny. Hereafter please let *me* provide plot and characters. By the way, where are you staying? I presume my actors located you without any trouble, but they haven't reported back yet."

"A joint called the *Potted Palm,*" I told him. "It's lousy with atmosphere. Also lousy, period. Any suggestions?"

"Take a beach cottage near by. If I recall my research, there's a place called Maracas Bay not far from town.

Hole up there for a few days until I have time to think what's going to happen to you next."

"Don't you *know*?"

"Frankly, no. You're beginning to sound like a producer—always insisting your own story gets priority. Yours isn't the only plot I'm juggling right now, you know. I'm working on five TV shows and two movies at the moment. Just relax and sit tight. Tight. That reminds me of a joke."

"To hell with your jokes. What I want to know is, is anybody else going to start throwing knives or lurking tonight—or can I expect a good night's sleep?"

"That depends on your conscience. And yes, I did contact someone else in Trinidad, a fellow—but let me tell my joke first. The joke is, why is a crazy Scotch girl great in bed? And the answer is, she's both wild and tight. Get it?"

"No," I said, honestly.

"I get it," said a strange female voice, "and I find it most offensive. This is the long distance operator, and I must caution you that telling offensive, obscene or suggestive jokes over the telephone is a federal offense."

"You lousy snooping operator!" yelled Barnaby. "Go automate yourself. I'll tell any jokes I feel like telling. Maybe I'll tell the one about the guy who dies and goes to hell, and the Devil shows him to his room—and there's this big bottle of whisky and a naked voluptuous blonde."

"Barnaby," I yelled, "I already *know* the joke."

"So do I," snapped the long distance operator. "And if he tries to tell the punch line I'm going to sever his connection."

"So this guy turns to the Devil," continued Barnaby relentlessly, "and says, 'you call this hell—a big bottle of whisky and a naked voluptuous blonde?' And the Devil says 'sure, because the *bottle* has a——' "

The line went dead.

"I warned him," gloated the long distance operator. "But no, he wouldn't listen. Now his connection's severed. *That'll* teach him—him and his offensive jokes."

"Look," I said, "Can't we——"

"And such *stupid* offensive jokes," continued the operator. "Who ever heard of a blonde without a——"

I hung up on her.

All the way back to the *Potted Palm* I found myself looking nervously from left to right and expecting the worst to come leaping from every shadow.

I wished I knew just who else in Trinidad Barnaby had told we were coming. And no doubt told to "jolly us up." A snake charmer? A lion tamer? A blow gun expert? A spear thrower? An explosives expert?

No telling.

Possibly no surviving, either.

However, the *Potted Palm* was still standing when I came up to it—I'd half expected to find a gutted crater—and when I'd climbed the creaking stairs to my room I found Sam, apparently intact also.

"Where've you been?" he asked. "I was worried something might have happened to you."

I was touched. "Why Sam," I said, "I wasn't sure you cared."

"Sure I care—if you get yourself knocked off how am I going to make contact with this Armenian character? Where did you run off to, anyway?"

"I was chasing a rumor," I said coldly. "It got away. And I noticed you didn't manage to catch En—that phantom sniper. Er, you *didn't* catch him, did you?"

Sam shook his head contritely.

"Bah. Only one sniper, and you——" I broke off. In the street below, a group of male voices broke into song.

*"Daaaay—Day O Day O O Day O O Daaaay!"* sang the voices.

We trooped to the window and peered out. A group of calypso singers clutching guitars were clustered below. "They must be about to sing the banana boat song," I said. "Funny coincidence that the opening line sounds like my name."

"They see us," noted Sam. "In fact they seem to have been waiting for us. Look, they're smiling and waving."

And so they were. But not for long. They almost immediately clutched their guitars, opened their mouths, and broke into song.

*O Jake of Arabia, we welcome thee*
*Back to the isle of La Trinitee*

"I'll be damned," said Sam. "They know you."

*From far Los Angeles you have returned*
*All Port of Spain is much concerned*

"I must admit," confessed Sam, "that I was beginning to doubt that you'd ever been to Trinidad before. But obviously I was wrong. You seem to be a local folk hero."

I shrugged modestly. Below us the calypso singers had a brief muttered conference before breaking into the next verse. Then they sang:

*What intrigue brings you we cannot guess*
*But we hope your dark mission is crowned with success*

I gritted my teeth. Surely Barnaby could have hired a more talented group than this. Dark mission indeed.

*O we're happy to hear you suffered no harm*
—sang our troubadors
*In the alley in back of the Potted Palm*
*Everybody!*
*O the villains they took it, on the lam*
*Pursued by Jake O'Day and a man named Sam*

"You're beginning to get famous yourself," I noted. Sam blushed happily.

*All hail to the hero of Trucial Kali*
*Who thwarts the Bulgarian's every sally*

"They seem to keep right up to date on what's going on," said Sam.

"I'll say," I agreed. "They must have just called Barn—I mean, I wonder how they knew about the Bulgarian?"

*But from now on, please, look both left and right*
*The Bulgarian may strike another night*
*For his heart is filled with villainy*
*And his methods are decidedly dastardly*

The calypso singers lowered their guitars and bowed.

"Throw them some coins," said Sam. "They seem to expect a tip."

"Anybody who rhymes *dastardly* with *villainy*," I snarled, "deserves nothing they get." Nevertheless I tossed down some coins before closing the window. Corny though the gimmick might be, I had to admit that Barnaby's prepaid serenade soothed my ego. At least now Sam would treat me with more respect—I hoped.

"A most interesting occurrence," Sam noted. "But doesn't it strike you that we seem to be attracting a bit too much attention?"

"You're right," I said. "Tomorrow let's rent a beach cottage some place—like Maracas Bay. It may be some days before the Armenian contacts us."

"Okay," said Sam. "It sure is frustrating not knowing what the Armenian wants us to do, though. I'd feel a lot better if I knew what was going to happen next."

"So," I agreed, "would I."

And with that we retired to our respective rooms and beds.

## Chapter 14

ONCE IN BED, however, sleep failed to come. I lay for a long while staring at the patched and peeling whitewashed ceiling, now splashed with reflected moonlight. Worrying.

I'm a natural worrier, I must admit, but that night I worried more than usual. For one thing, it worried me that Barnaby was not only plotting our 'adventure' long range, but was doing it more or less haphazardly—in between working on other plots.

What if he got his plots mixed up? What if he absentmindedly had us massacred by Indians or bandits? What if——

I got up, smoked a cigarette, finished the last of my Demarara rum and stared gloomily out into the dark, fragrant tropic night. A balmy breeze fanned my brow and from somewhere close by some kind of frog or bug or bird was cheeping softly and soothingly. It failed to sooth me, however. I kept waiting for the Creature from the Pink Lagoon to come slithering over the windowsill.

But that was just plain silly.

I went back to bed and lay counting pink lagoon creatures (in lieu of sheep) until finally I drifted off to sleep.

And that only made matters worse. Because naturally I dreamed . . .

In my dream I was eight feet tall and built like John Henry, and I strode like a conquering hero down the streets of Singakong—or was it Hongpore?—and men, women and pariah dogs fled yelping from my path.

I was dressed real sharp, too—sort of a cross between a White Hunter and Superman. With a hat like Gregory Peck wore in *The Macomber Affair.*

I stopped and beat my manly chest. "Anybody wanna rumble?" I yelled. Nobody did.

I pushed my way through a beaded curtain and found myself in a low tropic dive—just like in an old Glenn Ford-Rita Hayworth movie: smoke-filled and packed with exotic-looking extras.

I grabbed a bottle of rum from the bar, bit off the neck and took a swig. "It's Jake of Arabia!" screamed the bartender, and dived headfirst through the nearest window, red fez and all.

"It's Jake of Arabia!" chorused the male patrons, and began diving out the window after him. I checked them off as they dived by. Mike Hammer. Bulldog Drummond. Mr. Tamerlane. Shell Scott. Professor Moriarity and Holmes. Barnaby. Sam Spade. Phillip Marlowe. Dr. Bolingbrook. Nero Wolfe. Ellery Queen—in two parts. The 87th Precinct. And finally a shapeless pink creature that looked like it'd just crawled out of a lagoon.

Now I was alone—alone save for dozens of exotic-looking taxi dancers, naked save for their Maidenform bras. Some of them I recognized—Sugar, Mrs. Tamerlane the fourteenth, and Nancy Lou, my old girl from Wheat Rust, Kansas.

"Glad to see me, girls?" I yelled.

They were. They were so happy to see me they each jumped on a table and began to tap dance in unison—like in an old musical on the Late Show. I recognized the tune—The Sneak of Araby.

"Break it up girls!" I yelled. "This is an up-to-date movie."

They kept right on tap dancing, though—so I pushed my way out the back door, and all at once I was in a jungle clearing. A jungle girl stood before me, writhing sensuously. And what a girl.

She was naked save for a pink sarong, and since the sarong was wrapped around her head turban fashion it didn't obstruct my view. I watched fascinated as she writhed before me in ebony abandon, her thighs twin columns of erotic darkness, her breasts twin cones of gleaming jet, her belly a burnished bowl of midnight-hued flesh.

"Me Tondelayo," she murmured. "Me go for you big." She reached out a slender dark hand and ripped off my clothes. "Mmmm," she crooned, letting her dusky eyes slither up and down my body. "Want to get into my act?"

And all at once I was in her act. Also in her arms, my chest cushioned against the sooty suppleness of her full breasts, my abdomen in a close navel engagement with her tummy, my hands sliding down the resilient curve of her back to cup the great satiny globes of her inky buttocks.

Her luscious, lascivious flesh seemed to flow around me, over me, in a tide of erotic darkness . . . I was falling, falling, and she was falling on me like a soft tropical night. She was singing *Night and O'Day* as we fell. Even in my dream I winced. Corn is corn, even in Freudian symbols.

Suddenly our bodies were pulled rudely apart by a silver-haired Amazon. Not just silver-haired, either—she was silver all over: breasts, belly, backside—all of her glistened like she'd been chromium plated. A silvery sheen seemed to emanate from her queenly body.

"Me Queena, Sheen of the Jungle," she informed me. She smiled. "I think I can fit you into my act—at least for a one night stand."

"Your act isn't hot enough to get banned in Boston!" yelled Tondelayo. "Anyway, Jake prefers to team up with me." She turned to me. "Right?"

I backed away nervously.

"Well, speak up!" snapped the silver-skinned Amazon. "You can't be in both our acts at once. Which one of us do you like best?"

"I—I don't know," I stammered. "I'll have to call my script writer."

I turned and fled through the jungle. Behind me I could hear them pursuing me relentlessly, screaming with rage and frustrated passion. Faster and faster I fled, and faster and faster they pursued me—until suddenly the ground dropped out from under my feet and I was falling again.

Feet first into a Freudian jungle pool I fell, sinking down, down, down—into the arms of a mermaid. A blonde mermaid. She stuck her thumb into her mouth and giggled. Something about her looked familiar—perhaps it was the red belt she wore. But she was a real mermaid—below the hips she was all tail and a yard wide.

She smiled and wrapped her long mermaid tail around me and began to squeeze me tighter and tighter while I struggled wildly. Ever tighter she squeezed, and ever more wildly I struggled.

"That reminds me of a joke," I heard Barnaby say. "But first, a word from our sponsor——"

That woke me.

Which was too bad, in a way. Not that I care for commercials as a rule—but I'd liked to have known what kind of product was sponsoring a dream like mine.

Some rum company, most likely.

## Chapter 15

THE NEXT DAY I hired a car, hunted up a real estate agent, and rented us a cottage on Maracas Bay—a big, fairly isolated bungalow that sat right on the beach.

Looking back I can see that that wasn't very bright of me—renting the place, I mean. What I should have done was bought the cottage outright—in my name—and charged it off to expenses. Mr. Tamerlane was so rich he'd never have questioned it. Besides, in the tax bracket he was in it'd only have cost him a few cents.

And while I'm as honest as the next man, stealing a few cents hardly seems like stealing. Yeah, I should have bought the place. But I didn't, worse luck.

I also let Sam talk me out of hiring a red Jaguar convertible, which was what I had a fancy to do. Sam insisted we hire a black Austin sedan. Said it'd be less conspicuous in case we had to tail anybody.

A guy with a one track mind, Sam. No sense of fun.

Like, he approved of the beach cottage all right—but not because it was big and comfortable and well stocked (by me) with expensive canned foods and even more expensive bottled goods.

No, the reason he liked the place was because it was isolated.

"We could stand off an army here," he told me cheerfully. "Pick 'em off one by one as they came across the sand."

"Is that a fact?" I said.

"You bet. Isn't it about time we picked up some guns, Jake?"

"Uh, soon," I said. "No sense in rushing things. Besides, they might be hard to get. The British are sort of strict about firearms as I recall."

"Didn't you use any guns the last time you were in Trinidad?"

"Last time. Why, yes, of course. But, uh, that time I brought 'em with me." I looked around, like a conspirator. "Flew in a whole plane load."

"Why?"

Why? "How do I know why? Somebody paid me to is all I know." I smiled at my splendidly evasive answer.

"Who hired you?"

Who? Damn it, the kid was full of questions. Another evasive answer was called for. "In this business, Sam," I said, "it doesn't pay to ask too many questions." That, I figured, ought to hold him. It didn't.

"You mean you don't trust me, Jake?"

"No—I mean yes, of course."

"Then why won't you tell me who hired you to fly in guns the last time you were in Trinidad?"

Damn the boy. He really *did* have a one track mind. "If you want to know who hired me," I snapped, "it was the Bulgarian, that's who."

"The Bulgarian? I thought he was the sworn enemy of the Armenian—who's about to hire us now."

I smiled. A sinister smile. "So he is," I agreed. "But in this business, Sam, you learn to play both ends against the middle." I put a hard, brutal expression on my face. "Trust nobody—and betray everybody. That's my motto."

Sam stared at me with his cold, vacuous eyes. "I see. I must remember that. Betray everybody, eh?"

"Uh, present company excluded, of course," I said hastily.

"Of course," said Sam.

"Naturally I wouldn't betray you, Sam."

"Naturally."

"And naturally I don't expect you ever to betray me."

Sam smiled. A cold smile. About two hundred degrees below freezing. Real cold. "Naturally."

He sighed. "Certainly too bad we don't have any guns, though." He studied the cottage—we were sitting on the beach when this conversation took place—and said reflectively, "On the roof, I think. That'd be the best place."

"Best place for what?"

"For mounting a heavy-caliber machine gun. If we had a heavy-caliber machine gun. I'd put it smack in the middle, with sand bags all around. Then I'd cut a little hole in the roof, so's you could hand me up extra belts of ammunition."

"I could?"

"And grenades. If we had grenades. But a .50-caliber machine gun would be more fun."

"Uh, sure. Lots of laughs firing one of those."

"I can see it now," said Sam, his eyes half closed, a dreamy smile on his pimply face. "They start to sneak up on us, creeping across the sand. Suddenly *blam!* . . . *wham!* Two of 'em go shooting up in the air."

"Up in the air?"

"Yeah. 'Cause they've just touched off a couple of the land mines I've planted." He frowned. "Too bad we don't have any land mines. We could plant 'em all over the beach."

"Yeah," I said. "The tourists would get a big bang out of that."

Sam ignored me. "Then I'd open up with the machine gun. KA-BLAM-BLAM-BLAM-BLAM-BLAM! Cut 'em right in two."

"Uh, yeah. Undoubtedly."

Sam smiled. "Blood and intestines all over the place. KA-BLAM-BLAM-BLAM-BLAM-BLAM! Higher that time—bone and brains flying all over the beach. Can't you just see it, Jake?"

Unfortunately I could. I felt kind of sick to my stomach.

The next day I felt even sicker. I spent the morning loafing idly on the beach drinking beer. The afternoon I spent loafing and drinking rum. Sam had gone out in the car at noon. Sight-seeing, I'd presumed.

I was wrong. In the late afternoon he returned triumphantly brandishing two enormous revolvers.

"Webley .455's," he said happily. "Powerful enough to

knock a guy's head clean off his shoulders." He handed me one. I almost dropped it, it was so heavy. "I guess you know how to use one of these all right, eh Jake?"

"Oh, uh, sure," I said, holding the monstrous-looking weapon at arm's length. "Where'd you get 'em?"

Sam smiled. Enigmatically. "Asked around. In Urdu. Quite a few of the East Indians hereabouts speak Urdu. Good thing I studied it. Anyhow, I hinted around that I could use a couple of good sidearms—and eventually I got steered to this Urdu hock shop. That's where I bought 'em. Lucky, eh?"

He was lucky all right—lucky he hadn't been steered right into the local jail.

That evening I took the car and raced into town to call Barnaby. He seemed annoyed at being disturbed. "I haven't got to your plot yet," he told me. "Just sit tight for a few days and relax."

"How can I relax," I yelled long distance, "when that lunatic is going round brandishing a gun—two guns?"

"Well what do you want me to do—send you a target?"

"This is your adventure," I said. "Tell me how to fix the guns so they don't work. Or send me some blank cartridges air mail. As it is that crazy kid may shoot me in the back by mistake. Or not by mistake."

"Hmm. Well, you could monkey with the firing pins. But that's kind of tricky—and anyway, Sam might notice something was wrong."

"Mail me some blank cartridges, then."

"Tsk, tsk. Can't send cartridges through the mails—against the law."

I counted, slowly, to ten.

"Also," continued Barnaby—on the stroke of ten—"also blank cartridges are noticeable, too."

"They are?"

"Sure. Blanks have little wads of paper stuck in them instead of bullets. You ought to know that. What kind of a soldier of fortune are you, anyway?"

"An ersatz one. So what do I do?"

"Neutralize the shells he's got. Hold the line while I get one of my reference books and see how it's done."

Amazingly, he apparently had a book on just this subject, because a short while later he came back on the phone and gave me detailed instructions, which I carefully wrote down.

The next morning, while Sam was on the beach doing his daily push-ups, I set to work. First I fixed the shells in the gun he'd given me, then I put these dud shells in his gun and worked on the one's I'd taken from his, and finally I worked my way through a box of fifty spares he'd bought.

It was a long, tedious process enlivened only by my constant expectation of being blown up.

In case anyone is interested in how it's done, which I doubt, it involved using a couple of pairs of pliers to work each bullet carefully out of its shell—first wrapping the pliers in cloth to prevent leaving scratch marks. Then I dumped out the powder charge, poured a drop of water into the cartridge to wet the primer, and worked the bullet back into place.

Like I say, it was a long process, but by the time I finished I felt three hundred percent safer.

Even so, my efforts were nearly wasted. That afternoon Sam marched out onto the beach clutching his gun and a tin can. "Thought I'd try a little target practice," he informed me.

"You mean to say," I said quickly, "that a man your age isn't already an expert shot?"

Sam flushed. "Of course. Still, a little extra practice won't do any harm."

"You're right, Sam. But Sam, a gun that big probably makes a noise that can be heard a mile away, right?"

"Two miles," said Sam.

"There you are. Start firing off that cannon and we'll have the police on our necks. Also, the Bulgarian will learn that we're armed and will scare up a couple of artillery pieces to wipe us out at long range."

Sam nodded reluctantly. "I guess you're right, Jake. We'd better not use these guns except in an emergency." He marched back into the cottage—and for the second time that day I breathed easier.

Aside from the incident of the revolvers, however, the few days and nights we spent at the beach cottage were peaceful, sun drenched—and for me at least—pleasantly rum sodden. An oasis of calm between storms, you might say.

For one thing, Sam wasn't in my hair too much. During the day he drove the Austin around Trinidad casing escape routes and potential hide-outs—the idea of sightseeing for sightseeing's sake apparently never occurred to him.

("Visited Pitch Lake today."

"Oh?"

"Yeah. Great place for disposing of bodies—toss 'em in the asphalt and let 'em sink."

"Good. I'll keep it in mind."

Or—

"Checked out the Botanic Gardens this afternoon."

"Oh?"

"Yeah. I'm making a map of possible ambush sites."

"Good lad.")

While Sam conducted his lethal-minded excursions I toasted myself on the beach and experimented with various rum drinks. Evenings I took the car and drove in to Port of Spain to case the local night life on Frederick Street and along the water front. I always reported faithfully to Sam next morning:

"Cased a waterfront dive called The Bucket of Broads last night."

"Oh?"

"Yeah. No sign of the Bulgarian, worse luck—just dozens of exotic hostesses trying to get me drunk. They succeeded."

Or—

"Checked out the Orient Pearl Brothel last night. Sort of feeling out the lay of the land."

"Oh?"

"Yeah. Some of the girls tried to take me for a ride. They succeeded."

And so it went. Once or twice I tried, half-heartedly, to get Sam to accompany me on my nocturnal rambles. He always declined, however. One of us, he felt, should stay at the beach cottage at all times. In case the Armenian called.

At times, I must admit, I did feel twinges of guilt when I reflected on how much money I was making for doing nothing. I even, briefly, considered calling Sam's father and telling him he was wasting his money: Sam didn't crave exotic escapades—all he wanted was a chance to apply violence. Scientifically.

I didn't call, however. What the hell, Sam was having a good time planning massacres and ambushes. Me, I was just having a good time, period.

Which was how things stood when, five days after we'd rented the beach cottage, the Twins arrived.

## Chapter 16

THEY ARRIVED in sort of a spectacular fashion, too. Just after nightfall they came—and for once I was alone at the beach cottage while Sam was off night prowling. A good thing, too, all things considered.

The fact of the matter was that I was still more than a little hung over from my previous night's excursion in to Port of Spain and had decided to rest up a bit.

Sam returned from his day of reconnoitering around sundown and promptly launched into a detailed—and staggeringly blood-thirsty—exposition of his theory of guerrilla warfare. Boiled down, it amounted to a simple maxim: kill the enemy's women and children first. Slowly. And painfully.

"Sam," I said, taking a quick double gulp of rum, "why?"

"A matter of simple logic," Sam assured me. "You kill the opposition's women and children in a horrible fashion—and what happens? The opposition goes crazy with rage, that's what."

"This is good?"

"Of course. Get your enemy in a blind fury and he ceases to think and plan rationally. Then you can knock him off by means of scientifically applied violence."

"Yeah," I agreed. "After you wash all that blood off your hands, that is."

Naturally he took me literally. "A careful soldier of fortune," he assured me, "wouldn't get himself blood spattered. There are many, many ways to kill women and children without getting blood all over you. For instance——"

"Don't tell me," I begged.

He told me anyway.

I almost threw up.

One thing was certain—I wasn't going to spend a peaceful evening burying my hangover if Sam hung around talking about scientific violence. I decided to use strategy to get the creep out of the house.

"Sam," I said, "you told me the other day that you'd cased the Botanical Gardens for ambush sites we might use—but have you practiced finding these spots at night?"

"Gosh, no," admitted Sam, suddenly a young boy again. A blood-thirsty young boy. "Maybe I ought to, huh?"

"Certainly," I snapped. "It's the least you can do. Why don't you take the car and go do it now?"

"I will," said Sam, and off he went.

Alone at last, I mixed myself a local drink called (honest) Between-the-Sheets—a lethal mixture of rum, brandy, lemon juice and bitters—and began fiddling with a portable radio I'd bought, trying, futilely, to find a station that wasn't broadcasting the mistakes of some steel band.

It was then that the Twins burst into the cottage through the door that fronted on the beach. Like I say, it was kind of spectacular—and so were the Twins.

In the first place, they were Chinese, with exotic, Dragon-lady-type features. In the second place, they were soaking wet. In the third place, they were talking a mile a minute. And last—but positively not least—they looked as sexy as a five-foot shelf of pornography.

They were both wearing black silk Chinese dresses, the kind with the skirt slit up the side. *Way* up the side—like half-way to their waists. And the wet silk clung to the rest of their youthfully ripe young bodies like a coat of black paint. Thin black paint.

It clung so closely I could clearly see the tiny indentations that marked their navels—and every time they panted (which they were doing with great enthusiasm) their not-so-tiny nipples damn near shoved their way through the silk.

"Save us," gasped one, "from a fate worse than death!" gasped her twin.

"The Bulgarian," one panted . . .

"—was about to sell us," supplied the other—

"—into yellow slavery!"

They shuddered in unison.

"But we flung ourselves—"

"—off his yacht—"

"—and swam and swam—"

"—all the way to the shore—"

"—when we chanced to see your light—"

"—and here we are—"

"—at your mercy!"

They sank to their knees and clasped their hands together in mute but sexy supplication.

I groaned. I knew Barnaby well enough to recognize his corny lines only too well. "That's a dramatic story, girls," I said. "But unfortunately Sam isn't—"

"Don't throw us out!" they squealed in chorus.

"We don't know—"

"—where to turn."

"Also—"

"—we're broken—"

"—in spirit—"

"—and body."

"You don't," I told them, "look it."

"But—" pleaded one, "we've been swimming for hours and hours," supplied the other. "Through shark-infested waters—" "—fearing at any moment—"

"—to feel cruel teeth—" "—tearing at our soft young—"

"—bodies."

They shivered in tempo.

"Go away and swim back later," I said. "Sam isn't here right now."

They got to their feet angrily. "Well why in hell—" "—didn't you say so—" "—instead of letting us make—" "—fools of ourselves." They stamped their feet.

"Calm yourself girls," I said soothingly. "Cool down—or rather, warm up. You must be kind of chilly. Have some rum."

"Thank you," one said. "We don't mind if we do," concluded the other.

I mixed two more Between-the-Sheets. They drank cheerfully while sea-water dripped from their sodden dresses.

"Now," I said, "how did you *really* get here—and how did you get so wet?"

They looked at each other, nodded, looked at me, smiled. "We took a cab." And had the driver let us out down the road." "Then we walked along the beach." "Until we got real close." "Then we dunked ourselves in the ocean." "And here we are."

"That," I said, "is about what I figured. I suppose Barnaby hired you long distance?"

They nodded.

"And those were Barnaby's lines you were spouting—about the Bulgarian and all?"

They looked sheepish. "In a manner of speaking." "But we improved his script a little." "To make it more dramatic." "That's because secretly we've always wanted—" "—to be actresses." "Dramatic—" "—actresses."

I sighed. "I sort of figured acting wasn't your line. What do you do normally?" A pang of alarm swept through me. "You aren't knife throwers by any chance?"

"Of course not."

"We strip."

"Like this—"

And with that they began to wriggle and slither out of their wet dresses, their dainty Oriental hands darting to identical matched zippers.

"But of course—"

"—usually we strip—"

"—more slowly."

"And to music."

"There!"

"Do you—"

"—like us?"

I stared, a little dazed, at their nude, wet and shining golden bodies and nodded weakly. Like them? Hell, they looked good enough to eat—two succulent, spicy Oriental dishes. Tender looking, too.

They weren't especially big girls—but neither were they as diminutive as Sugar. They were just, well, normal-sized girls. In height. Contour-wise they were built like a pair of brick pagodas.

To my way of thinking, there are few sexier looking objects in the world than a voluptuous Oriental girl. When a Caucasian girl is voluptuous she's apt to be voluptuous all over—if you know what I mean: if she has ripe, deliciously full thighs, her calves are likely to be rather

full too. If her bosom sticks out far enough so that she has trouble going through a doorway sideways, and her hips are wide enough to keep her out of phone booths, then her waist and upper arms are apt to be a wee bit chubby, too.

Not that I mind all that much, of course. I like plenty of girl flesh—within reason—wherever and whenever I find it.

But Oriental girls, let's face it, have a sort of built-in feminine grace and daintiness—a kind of slender, lithe suppleness to their bodies.

And when this slender litheness is combined—as it was with the Twins—with full, firm, up-jutting breasts; with insolently flaring hips; with ripely saucy buttocks; and with lushly fleshed thighs—the total effect would turn a choir boy into a drooling satyr.

What I mean is, it kind of hits you smack in the hormones.

And it wasn't just one sexy, lithe-yet-voluptuous golden-bodied nude Oriental chick I was gaping at but two, count them, two of the cutest, most torrid-shaped chicks that had ever stripped themselves before my delighted eyes.

"Wow," I said. Reverently.

"I guess," said one of the Twins, "he likes us." "Or he wouldn't be drooling," opined the other.

I closed my mouth hastily. Damn it, I *was* drooling. But with good reason. Then I remembered my manners. "Uh, would you girls like a towel—or do you want to just drip-dry?"

They thought about that. Their method of consulting was to lower their heads and stare at each other blank faced. Either through some telepathy or else long familiarity with their own mutual thought processes, they seemed able to conduct lengthy silent discussions that way.

This discussion was short, however. They turned to me, raised all four of their eyebrows and said: "Perhaps we could use—" "—your shower." "So as to wash the salt—" "—off us."

"Uh, sure," I said. "This way."

I led them into the beach cottage's bathroom which boasted, as it happened, a shower stall big enough to stable a horse in. My two new found golden ponies trotted into it, wrestled with the taps, squealed shrilly when the cold water came on, then adjusted the temperature and began to soap themselves.

I watched fascinated as four golden hands soaped two golden waists, lathered four golden breasts, rubbed soap over dual golden bellies, scrubbed two pairs of shining golden thighs.

It struck me that I was neglecting my duties as host: "Anything I can do to help, girls?" I asked. "Scrub your backs—or something?"

The Twins giggled and lifted their long black hair out of their eyes. Apparently they didn't need to consult each other this time. They simply smiled and chorused: "We'd *like* that."

I turned my back modestly while I ripped off my clothes. Then I stepped into the shower. What a wise, far-seeing architect it'd been who'd designed this particular shower stall—doubtless he (or perhaps she?) had foreseen that there might come a time when a guy and two dolls might wish to do a little community bathing.

I lathered soap suds on my hands and said, "What are you girls called?"

"Well," said one, "Barnaby told us we should call ourselves Yin and Yang, for some reason." "But," said the other, "our real names are Joy." "And Toy."

"Which is which?" I asked, rubbing soap suds onto Joy (or Toy)'s back.

Silence.

"Well?" I queried.

That bought me two snickers. "We'd rather not tell," said the chick who's back I was soaping. "That way," said the other, "if one of us does something unlady-like, the other one won't get blamed."

My interest—already fairly high—began to climb even higher. "You mean one of you is a shameless hussy?"

"Right," they said together.

"And the other one?"

"She's a slut."

Things certainly did sound promising. They felt promising, too. There seemed to be an infinity of erotic promises in the sleek, sloping golden curves of Joy (or Toy)'s now nicely lathered body.

Up the sleek golden cliff of her shoulders slid my soapy

hands, then down the golden curve of her spine to lathe the bouncing golden spheres of her buttocks.

Bouncing?

Yes, bouncing. Some girls can make their buttocks bounce up and down while they themselves stand still. Toy (or Joy) obviously had admirable muscular control.

She had great—if impudent—muscular control as well. Her soapy golden buttocks twitched and quivered under my soapy hand the way a horse's rump does when its trying to shake loose a fly.

"Me too," said her twin, and I felt up—I mean washed —her as well.

Maybe you think I was overdoing the gracious host bit —that I should have let the girls perform their own soapy ablutions. That, in short, I was letting myself be imposed upon.

If you think that, it only goes to prove that you've never washed a pair of wriggling, laughing Chinese girls. Its an admirable indoor sport, believe me. A hobby I wholeheartedly recommend to every man who ever feels a need of . . .

Well, who just feels the need. Or just likes to feel.

"Frontsides next," sang out my golden girls—and stood expectantly back to back. Back to back like bookends they stood. It made it much easier for me to soap their dual frontsides simultaneously.

It also made them look erotic as—well, you can imagine how erotic they looked standing that way. They felt even more that way. When I closed my eyes it gave me the damndest feeling to soap them—like I was soaping one girl with four breasts, mounted bow and stern. Or port and starboard, depending upon how you thought of it.

Me, I didn't think. I just kept my eyes closed and worked soap suds over them. There was something temptingly improper about the way their saucy, impudent young breasts responded to my soapy caress. Their breasts seemed almost to flirt with me—to duck and squirm out of my grasp only to bob up again for me to catch them once more.

"Mmmmmm—*mmmm*!" said the Twins. And then, "Now its *our* turn."

"All right girls," I said. "I'm all yours."

And they started soaping me. Four slender, teasing, soapy hands slid everywhere, but everywhere over my body. Twenty golden fingers left twenty trails of sexual ecstasy—and soap—over my tingling wet flesh.

Around and round they soaped me, up and down and from side to side they worked. Only from the way they were giggling and laughing they didn't seem to think of it as work. Neither did I.

Pretty soon, though, I figured they'd soaped me enough. "That's plenty, girls," I told them.

Then we rinsed ourselves off and, without bothering to dry ourselves (it was a hot night anyway) went into my bedroom and collapsed on the bed.

## Chapter 17

SOME TIME AFTER—I don't, I'm sure, need to explain after *what*—I decided it was time to talk business.

Since I was lying in the middle of the bed and Joy and Toy were lying close along either side of me, I was in a convenient position to confer with them. A comfortable position, too.

My right arm was under Toy (or Joy)'s back, my right hand comfortably cupped over her outboard breast and my left arm and hand occupied a similar position in relation to Joy. (Or Toy.) And on both sides my body was pressed against sleekly and hotly by their tired young bodies. I was pretty tired myself, for that matter. Doubly tired. Remember there were two of them and only one of me. All three of us had expressed regret concerning this a number of times since we'd first collapsed on the bed.

However . . .

To business. "Just what," I asked, "did Barnaby tell you to do—or say? I mean, what part are you supposed to play in this adventure?"

"What adventure?" they asked.

A good question. "Let me put it this way," I said.

"Which way? Which way? Have you thought of a new——"

"No!" I snarled. "Get your hot little thoughts off sex. I'm being verbal right now. What I mean is, what instructions did Barnaby give you?"

"Oh. That. Well, he called us long distance. In Miami. That's where we were working. In a night club. Stripping. And then we quit. Because Barnaby said he'd pay us *enormous* sums of money. For playing sort of a joke. On a loony. Named Sam."

"That's my boy," I said.

"So we said sure, and what did we have to do, and Barnaby said whatever sexy things came into our heads, so naturally lots of sexy things came into our heads right off, so we told Barnaby some of these, and Barnaby kept saying *wow* and *gee* and *I wonder if I can teach Sugar to do that,* and so on, and then this operator came on the line and threatened to sever Barnaby's connection again if we didn't stop talking that way, so we stopped."

"I see," I said, feeling a little confused. One reason I was somewhat confused was that the Twins persisted in talking alternately—the end result was a (reasonably) coherent sentence, but until I got used to their way of talking I kept moving my head back and forth like I was watching a tennis match.

After a while, though, I got so it didn't bother me. Talking to the Twins got to be just like talking to one person. In stereo.

"So all we really know," continued the Twins, "is that we're supposed to be fleeing from someone called the Bulgarian. And you and your loony friend——'

"Sam," I supplied.

"You and your loony friend Sam are supposed to offer us succor."

"What?"

"Succor. Like you'll take us under your protection. And then ravish us. Hour after hour. Night after night. Which sounds like fun. *Lots* of fun."

"Yeah." It did at that. "And you don't play any other part in the plot—I mean, that's all you're supposed to do? Just hang around acting sexy and frightened?"

"That's right," they chorused. "Barnaby said, and we quote, that we are to play the part of red herrings, unquote. Also, we quote further, we're to serve to keep things simmering until Barnaby has time to work out something more definite plot-wise. End of further quote."

Just as I'd suspected. Barnaby had given Sam and my adventure a low priority. He was too busy plotting his stupid television shows to plot anything adventurous for us. Still, I had to admit that Joy and Toy were pretty tasty-looking red herrings. And it'd been thoughtful of Barnaby to hire twins so that I could have a ball as well as—

Sam.

"Girls," I said slowly, "there's one little thing which I should mention. It's something Barnaby didn't foresee. Something I didn't foresee. Hell, no normal person could have foreseen it."

"What?"

"Sam. His attitude towards sex. He has a—a rather unique attitude towards sex."

"Yes? Yes? What does he do? Come on, tell us. He's got a new kick worked out? Something awful—but nice?"

"Well——"

"What does he *do*?"

"He doesn't."

Silence. Then, "Not at all? Not even once or twice a night? Not *ever*?"

"So far as I can determine—or guess—no. He has a theory about sex. Says it saps the strength."

"Well *sure,*" said the Twins. "Of *course.*" A dual giggle. "But like who *cares*?" Another dual giggle. "You can sap our strength *any* time."

"Thank you," I said sincerely. "And I enjoyed the way you sapped mine."

"Any time," said the Twins. "Time after time." They wriggled closer against me. "Be sure to let us know," they added, "the moment you feel your sap—that is your strength—rising again."

"Soon, I hope. Uh uh—don't grab. Not *that* soon. But getting back to Sam."

"Oh, *him*. We don't like him. Even without meeting him we don't like him."

"You show good judgement," I agreed. "But the fact remains that you were hired—at least half of you was hired—to vamp Sam. To sex him up in an adventurous, exotic way. And since Sam doesn't play that way—well, it sort of complicates things. I guess."

"Not," said the Twins, "at all. We'll just sex *you* up twice as often."

"That, I said, "might be the best solution." I stretched myself luxuriously on the bed.

"Now?" they queried.

"Soon," I promised. "By the way, you never told me just what kind of a strip act you do."

"No," they agreed, "we didn't."

I waited. "Well?"

Silence. Then another dual giggle. Then more silence. Then, "Shall we tell him?" they asked each other. They considered. "Let's," they decided. They told me.

"Good *grief*!" I said, startled into sitting bolt upright. "Nice girls like you do a thing like *that*?"

"You bet," they assured me. "Over and over. We *like* doing it in fact." A double giggle. "And anyway, we aren't really nice girls. Certainly not. Who wants to be a nice girl?"

"Still," I said, shaking my head, "an act like that——"

"We only do that at stags actually. For night clubs we have a *much* different act. Clean. Wholesome. A treat for the whole family. The Jukes and Sykes family."

"Like what?"

They told me.

I gasped. "You call that a wholesome act? That's the most licentious, lascivious, lewd, improper, immoral——"

I paused for breath.

"That's what the judge said last week," said the Twins. "And *he* paused for breath, too. We felt sure we were going to jail. For years and *years*. But it was okay."

"It was?"

"Yes. We asked to speak to the judge in his chambers. Then we did our stag act for him. And on him. And over him. And sort of slithering around him. He had a ball. So did we. He fined us ten dollars was all. And he paid the fine himself. And bought us lunch. He was a *nice* judge."

"Uh, yes, I'm sure he was. But just because he was a pushover for your wanton wiles, don't think you can pull any of those licentious, lascivious, lewd and improper tricks on me."

The twins sat up and stared at me. Licentiously. "Why not?" they asked.

"Why—" I said. I stopped. I couldn't think of a good reason, why not.

So the Twins did their stag act for me. And on me. And over and under me. And slithering all around me. It was a long act, the way they did it—and they did it with diabolical attention to details. My details. For ten minutes they worked, twenty, twenty-five . . .

And then the pressure in my metaphorical boiler passed the point of human endurance and I shoved one twin ungraciously off the bed and flung myself upon the other. Our bodies came together frantically, passionately.

Her slender arms wound themselves around my back and her soft thighs and lower legs imprisoned my body, pulling me deep into the throbbing pulse of her flesh.

The room seemed to dissolve into a kaleidoscope of multicolored desire . . . nothing existed save the throbbing contact of flesh with flesh, the ever mounting, all but unbearable, agonizing ecstasy of skyrocketing passion . . .

And then the fires of hell and the rivers of heaven seemed to pulse as one through my body—and in one, two, three, four, five seconds it was over.

Time passed.

Don't ask me how much time—I was in another universe, a tired, sleepy, spent, satiated universe. For all I know ice ages might have come and gone, empires risen and fallen. Dimly, numbly, I tried to think. Was that an empire rising and falling beneath me? No, it was a girl gasping for breath.

Vaguely, semi-consciously I was aware that she was wriggling away from me. Suddenly, alarmedly, I realized that another girl was wriggling toward me from the other side.

"Now me," said the other girl.

"No," I gasped, "no, no, *no*!"

The other girl wriggled herself into a more comfortable position. "Yes," she said, "absolutely. Come on, Jake. You can do it."

And believe it or not I did.

## Chapter 18

WHEN I AWOKE the next morning I had the vague but vivid memory of a curious dream—a dream in which I'd spent a good part of the night plunging in and out of a sea of golden flesh.

Then I opened my eyes and realized I hadn't been dreaming. In the morning sunlight, sprawled sleepily on my bed, Joy and Toy looked like erotic statues cast in gold. Soft, malleable gold . . .

How many times had I alloyed myself with them? I counted. Good *grief!* I counted again and reached the same staggering total. No wonder I was tired all over.

My arms were tired, my legs were tired, my lips were tired, and—well, like I said, I was tired all over. One part in particular was almost numb. (My left arm—in case you're curious: one of the Twins had evidently been sleeping on it.)

I thought about waking the Twins and— No. I didn't have the strength.

So I simply crawled out of bed and into the shower, moaned under the cold water for a few minutes, then dressed and staggered into the kitchen.

Sam was busy making a pot of coffee.

"The damndest thing, Jake," he said. "There are two Chinese silk dresses lying on the living room floor."

"That's nothing," I said, pouring myself a cup of black coffee. "Just wait until you see what's lying on my bed. Two Chinese chicks."

Sam stared at me with a riled surmise for a moment, then walked off to investigate. I gulped four cups of black coffee while he was gone. I needed every cup.

"Amazing," said Sam when he returned a few moments later. "Where did they come from?"

Where? "Why—" I stopped. Suddenly it didn't seem like a good idea to tell Sam the story Barnaby had cooked up.

*They say they're fleeing from the Bulgarian.*

*Bah! A likely story. Most likely they're his spies.*

*Nonsense—two cute little chicks like that?*

*They don't look cute to me—they look like spies. But don't worry—I'll choke the truth out of them . . .*

He was just capable of doing it, too.

"What's the matter?" asked Sam. "Why are you staring at the wall and moving your lips soundlessly?"

"I was conducting a mental dialogue with you—I mean with myself,"I said.

Sam looked at me strangely. "Oh. Well, to repeat, who are they?"

"They're two Chinese-American strippers I met," I said truthfully. "I invited them to stay with us for a while."

"Bah!" said Sam. "Why?"

I shook my head sadly. "If you don't know, already Sam, nobody—but nobody—could make you understand."

"What's to understand?" demanded Sam.

"Sam," I said, "didn't you notice what cute, saucy, impudent breasts they had?"

He nodded. "Of course. What's so unusual about that? All females of the species *Homo sapiens* have mammaries. Their mammaries seemed to be somewhat larger than average, I'll admit—but not abnormally so."

"Sam," I said wearily, "didn't you notice what ripe, full hips they had—what insolently plump buttocks—what wonderfully firm but soft thighs?"

"Sure," said Sam. "All girls are like that anatomically. It's on account of layers of fatty material under their epidermis."

"Sam," I snarled, "go soak your head in the ocean!"

Sam blinked. "What for?"

I counted to ten. Slowly. Then I said, "Why, to toughen your scalp of course. You know, the way prize fighters soak their hands in brine to harden their fists. A professional soldier of fortune ought to have a tough scalp as a defensive measure—in case he gets bopped on the head by a coffee pot—I mean a gun butt."

"Oh," said Sam, "I'll have to try it."

And I'll be damned if he didn't. Unfortunately he failed to drown himself.

Later that morning I drove to the airport and picked

up the Twin's suitcases which they'd checked there. I also called Barnaby.

"Your two Chinese strippers arrived in good shape," I told him. "What do I do with them?"

"Tsk, tsk," said Barnaby. "If you and Sam don't know already, nobody, but——"

"*Aside* from that," I yelled. "I mean, how long are they supposed to stay and all that?"

"Oh. Hold the line a minute while I check my plot sheet for this caper." I held the line. "Three days," said Barnaby a moment later. "After that I'm shifting your locale. I've been using Trinidad as a background too much lately; I'm getting tired of it."

"Where," I asked, "are you shifting us to?"

Barnaby chuckled. "I'll surprise you."

Which probably meant he hadn't gotten around to deciding.

"What do you think of Joy and Toy?" he asked. "Cute, eh?"

"Yeah," I said grudgingly, "Not bad. Kind of wild, in fact."

Barnaby snorted. "If you think *they're* wild you ought to meet the two Cherokee chicks I intended to ship you, only I found out they were in jail in Grand Rapids on a morals charge. They're *really* wild. I understand their grandmother made a man out of Billy the Kid—and their great-grandmother was reputedly responsible for most of Custer's last stands."

"This is the long distance operator," said a female voice. "I don't like the drift of this conversation one bit."

"What's wrong with my conversation?" yelled Barnaby. "I was only telling Jake about a female Indian warrior who liked to waylay paleface soldiers. All along the way she'd la——"

The line went dead.

Barnaby and his big mouth.

I drove back to the beach cottage. And there I stayed. With the Twins. I was sometimes amazed at my staying power, in fact. The four of us—Sam, the Twins and I—quickly settled down to a new routine.

In the mornings Sam would go out on the beach and do push-ups while the Twins and I stayed indoors and did somewhat similar exercises. Afternoons Sam took the car and explored the island, while I took a nap and then explored the Twins.

Evenings Sam went to bed and read. The Twins and I went to bed, too—but what with one thing and another we didn't do much reading.

And so the days and nights passed. Pleasantly if exhaustingly. Never before had I been so tiredly content. Life, in fact, would have been just about perfect—but for Sam.

While the Twins and I swilled rum and sinned incessantly in the sun, Sam sat around looking coldly disapproving.

"Jake," he told me several times, "you're sapping your strength beyond all reason."

I told him what to do.

"I'm doing that regularly," he complained. "And all it does is make my scalp itch. Also I get sea water in my ears."

You can see how a guy like that would bug you.

He bugged the Twins, too. But while to me Sam was just a juvenile pain in the neck, to the Twins—lusty young females that they were—he was something else: a challenge.

They explained this to me on the morning of the third day after their arrival, the day on which they were scheduled to fly back to the States to fulfill a stag engagement in Memphis.

"Well," I told them, "if he's such a challenge to you, why haven't you tried to seduce him?"

"We have," they told me. "Over and over. While you were out. Or sleeping. It didn't take." They sighed. "I," said one, "even climbed in bed with him. He climbed out."

"And I," said the other, "took a shower with him. I got clean. Period."

"A real challenge," I agreed.

"But we're not through," they told me, "yet. We have," they confided, "a plan."

"What?"

They told me.

"It's an idea," I admitted. "But kind of dangerous, don't you think? What if he got loose?"

"Leave that," they said, "to us. We've got the rope all ready."

"Well, okay," I said. "What do you want me to do?"

"Nothing. Just go away for—" they considered "—about two hours. That ought to be *plenty* of time."

So I took the car and drove in to Port of Spain and sampled rum concoctions for a couple of hours. When I drove back the Twins, fully dressed, were standing outside the cottage with suitcases in hand. Never had I seen two more crestfallen, defeated looking chicks.

"Drive us," they requested me mournfully, "to the airport. Please. And quickly. We want to leave—" they glanced morosely over their shoulders "—the scene of our humiliation."

On the way to the airport they told me what had happened.

"We dropped the noose over him without any trouble," they said gloomily, "and had him tied up in no time. Then we tied him onto the bed. Facing upwards. Then we set to work."

"What did you do?"

They told me. In graphic detail.

"Wow," I said. "That's better—or at least as good—as anything you did to me. That *must* have gotten a rise out of him. It did, didn't it?"

The Twins didn't answer. They didn't have to. The look of utter defeat on their faces told me the answer: their most wanton wiles had been wasted on Sam.

I saw them on to their plane—two broken sex-pots—and drove back to the cottage to untie Sam.

"Jake," he gasped, after he'd pulled the gag from his mouth, "those girls *were* spies after all. The moment you left the cottage they jumped me, tied me to the bed and started torturing me."

"Is that a fact?" I said, opening a fresh bottle of rum.

"Fact. They used all kinds of subtle Oriental tortures—like, well like tickling me with feathers. Only they didn't use feathers."

"I can imagine," I said. I could, too. A shiver of reminiscence ran through me.

"They kept it up for *hours*. You wouldn't *believe* some of the things they did to me."

"Oh yes I would," I said dreamily, taking another belt of rum.

"But I held out. No matter what they did, I didn't move a muscle. You'd have been proud of me, Jake."

"Yeah, proud." I swigged more rum. "Sam," I said, "Sam, did it ever occur to you that perhaps they had something else in mind—that they weren't exactly trying to torture you?"

"Don't be ridiculous," said Sam. "Of course they were—they were trying to torture the truth of the matter out of me, that's what."

"Sam," I said between gulps of rum, "just what *is* the truth of the matter?"

Sam scratched his scalp. Doubtless because it itched. "Gosh," he admitted, "come to think of it, I don't know."

Somehow I had the feeling he never would, either.

Next morning we found a note—written in a poor facsimile of blood—pinned to the front door of the cottage by a stiletto.

*Trinidad is getting too hot for me,* read the note. *Fly at once to Mexico City. Further instructions there. (Signed) The Armenian.*

So off we went to Mexico City.

## Chapter 19

In Mexico City I fell in love.

Mexico City, according to the guide books, has a population in excess of 4,000,000—making it the fourth largest city in the western hemisphere and the tenth largest in the world. It has an ideal climate, has an average altitude of 7,500 feet, and was conquered by Cortes in 1521.

Built on the site of a former lake, it is flanked to the southeast by two volcanoes named Popocatepetl and Ixtacihuatl, neither of which I can pronounce.

It's also a real swinging town, a great place for fanciers of bullfights and booze, beautiful buildings and bosomy broads.

But I don't remember Mexico City for any of these things—I remember it as the town where I fell in love.

Not for the first time, to be sure. Like the song says, I've been in love before.

But never, never so completely, totally, so incandescently, so rhapsodically. Never—but I'm getting ahead of my story.

The flight from Port of Spain to Mexico City was uneventful; both Sam and I spent most of the time studying guidebooks— I didn't bother, this time, pretending that I was an old Mexico City hand; it was too damn much trouble. And anyway, no one could expect even a top-notch soldier of fortune to be familiar with *every* foreign city.

So I spent my time in flight studying guide books. Most of the time, at least; part of the time I devoted to studying the plane's air hostess—a pert-faced, olive-skinned chick whose bra was stuffed to the bursting point with olive-hued breast flesh that made my fingers itch to play lucky dip. A living doll, our hostess.

It wasn't, however, with her that I fell in love.

At the airport I hailed a taxi and told the driver to take us to the best hotel in town—the hell with atmosphere and intrigue; I felt like living in style. The driver nodded and asked if we'd like to take a little joy ride first.

Sam declined for us before I could open my mouth. He had, he explained in a stage whisper, an urgent need to visit a bathroom. He would.

So we didn't take a joy ride. A pity. The driver of the taxi was a raven-haired beauty with high, jutting cheekbones that bespoke Aztec blood and high, jutting breasts shaped like scale models of Ixtacihuatl and Popacatepetl. No doubt she would have provided a lively, joyful ride.

It wasn't, however, with her that I fell in love.

Nor did I fall in love with the desk clerk at *Chez Cortes,* the luxury hotel at which we stayed—though she was lovable enough, with her startlingly contrasting dark skin and naturally blonde hair.

Her coloring made her look oddly like a photographic negative, and I longed to know what might develop if I got her in a dark room. I didn't, however, fall in love with her.

Nor did I fall in love with the bell girl—a vast improvement over the bell boy system—who carried our baggage to our suite, though she was pretty cute baggage in her own right. Nor did I lose my heart to the playful eyed chambermaid whose hips hinted—in body Spanish—that she'd as soon make me as my bed. Nor—but you get the idea.

And in case you're wondering why I'm bothering to catalog the maidens I failed to fall in love with, it's simply because I want to make it clear that I don't go around falling in love with just *any* gorgeous chick. Since the doleful episode of Nancy Lou, in fact, I'd developed—I thought—a total immunity to love. Not sex, love; no one is immune to sex.

Except Sam.

But I digress. To continue my tale chronologically, after we'd been shown to our suite and Sam had scurried into the bathroom, I dumped my suitcase and took the elevator back down to the lobby, intending to call Barnaby and hoist a few drinks in that order.

She was sitting in the lobby.

Alone, in a vast chair that made her seem impossibly doll-like and tiny, she sat with her back straight and her knees decorously together, her tiny hands folded in her lap.

I noticed her, idly, the moment I stepped out of the elevator. I always noticed good-looking girls, and this one looked better than most. Still, I wasn't in love with her. Not then.

I strolled across the lobby towards the telephones and glanced at her, casually, again. At closer range I could see that she was very young, seventeen or eighteen perhaps, and that her hair was very long and soft and copper-red, her eyes huge and fawn-like, her skin the color of fresh poured cream.

Even then I wasn't in love with her—I wasn't even giving her my full attention; part of my mind was devoted to what I was going to say to Barnaby, and part to whether I should stick to rum or try some tequila drinks. I certainly wasn't thinking about falling in love; I wasn't even thinking, consciously, about trying to pick her up.

Some of my reflexes—especially those related to sex—are fully automatic, however. Hence, without consciously willing my feet to steer in her direction, I found myself angling across the lobby headed directly towards her.

I noted, almost dispassionately, that her silk-stockinged legs—what I could see of them at least—were trim and shapely; that her waist was youthfully slender, her breasts unusually high and zestfully up-tilted.

Then our eyes met—and it happened.

All right, already. I know this all sounds cornball—but that's the way love is: the stuff clichés as well as dreams are made of; silly, impossible, improbable and unlikely is love.

Her eyes—her huge, vividly green eyes—met mine and we stared for a fraction of a second deep into each other's souls and my soul smiled at hers and hers—wonder of wonders—smiled back.

If you've never been in love, you're quite welcome to disbelieve anything like that could happen. I wouldn't have believed it myself, a second before it happened. But then again, maybe it *has* happened to you, maybe you too once fell in love, a decade or a day ago, and you felt as I did.

Maybe you, too, heard a mushy string orchestra playing *Some Enchanted Evening* in your head; maybe you also felt happy and sad and sentimental and shook up all at once—the way I did at three seventeen P.M. in the lobby of a hotel in Mexico City.

For a moment I stood, sort of rocking unsteadily on my feet, wondering what had hit me. Then my mental background music—still strings—quieted enough so that I could hear myself think, and I thought. *Hot damn,* I thought. Also *wow* and *zowie* and *holy cow* and *how do I love thee, let me count the ways* and similar crazy things.

Aloud I said, "Uh, are you waiting for someone, Miss?"

Pretty trite, I admit—but I was still too shook-up to think up a more original approach. I should have done better, nevertheless. *Are you waiting for someone?* is one of the worst pick-up lines there is—it invites too many varieties of cutting rejoinders. The instant I voiced it I cursed to myself and waited for her lip to curl in scorn as she prepared to cut me and my crude approach down to size.

Her lip didn't curl, however. Instead it quivered slightly and her huge eyes filled suddenly with tears.

"I—I was," she said. And then she lowered her face and began, almost silently, to cry.

"Here, here," I said. "It can't be as bad as all that can it? Or can it?"

She said nothing, just sat there with great tears coursing down her exquisite cheeks.

What next? "Uh, is there something I can do?" I asked. "*Any*thing I can do?"

She shook her head silently: no.

Then, very quietly, "Please—please go away. I—I know you're trying to be helpful but—but there's nothing you can do. Nothing—nothing anyone can do."

Put down this way in black and white, these words she spoke sound, well, ordinary. Conventional. The kind of words any girl sitting in a hotel lobby crying to herself might say.

But she wasn't just any girl, and I wasn't seeing her words in black and white, I was hearing them spoken in a soft, contralto voice that—well, it tore my heart out was what it did.

All the sadness of disillusioned youth, all the depthless melancholy of the self-damned was in her voice; in her muted tones echoed the bewildered hurt of all young girls who have Stooped to Folly—and gotten kicked from behind emotionally.

Because it was quite obvious, to my alert brain, that she had Stooped to Folly. Like, she was wearing a cheap gold ring on her third finger, a ring that didn't fit. That meant she'd been spending a week or a weekend pretending to be somebody's wife.

That was one thing. Another was the simple fact that she was sitting waiting for someone who hadn't come—who undoubtedly wasn't going to come. Her parents—some relative? Hardly. If that had been the case she would have simply marched up to the hotel desk and made inquiries—or gone to the Mexican equivalent of Traveler's Aid.

No, she was waiting—had been waiting—for a man. A man who had done her wrong. Over and over, no doubt. And had a ball every time, most likely. The swine.

"Look," I said, "you can't just sit here."

She continued to weep, silently.

"Do you need money?"

She shook her head.

"Any plans?"

She raised her giant, tear-filled green eyes to my face and slowly nodded.

"What plans?" I asked.

She told me her plans.

"Where?" I asked.

She looked a little startled. "Does—does it matter where?"

"Sure it does," I said (trying, as you may have guessed, to snap her out of her mood), "it matters a whole lot. If you killed yourself here in the lobby you'd make a mess all over the carpet. It would upset the hotel management—undermine Mexican-American relations.

"Far be it from me to try and change your mind," I added quickly before she could speak. "You want to kill yourself—that's your business. All I'm trying to do is be helpful. Most likely you don't realize it, but killing one's self isn't easy. Guns are hard to buy. Knives are tricky to use. Poison doesn't always work. And as for jumping in front of a bus—" I shook my head. "Very risky."

She blinked. "Risky?"

"Sure. Only a small percentage of people who jump in front of buses get killed quickly and neatly. Suppose you jumped in front of a bus—and then woke up in a hospital bed with all your arms and legs in traction splints. It'd be an awful anticlimax. You'd feel like a fool."

She looked at me blankly for a long moment, her face streaked with tears. Then the corners of her beautiful mouth crooked into a smile. A tiny smile, but a smile.

"Let's have no levity," I said severely. "This is a serious business. Suicide is one of the most important steps a young girl makes in her life—a step the wise girl plans carefully in advance."

I reached down and took one of her hands, tugged gently. "Come on," I said, "let's adjourn to the hotel bar and have a couple of drinks while we decide the best way to knock you off."

For a moment she resisted me. Then suddenly she smiled and rose from her chair. "You're crazy," she said. "But——"

"But likable," I finished. "All my friends say that.

Jake, they say, may be a lunatic—but you can't help liking the bastard. I feel the same way."

"You *are* crazy," she said as I led her towards the bar, "you really are. But—but thank you for being crazy. If you know what I mean."

I steered her into a dimly lit booth and ordered a brace of double brandies. Ten minutes later I ordered a second round. Between rounds she alternately dabbed at her face with my handkerchief and poured out her sad story.

It was just about as I'd figured. "We—my parents and I—were in Acapulco. On vacation. And then—and then I met this man. On the beach. My parents didn't like him, said he was too old for me. Only he was such a nice man—didn't make a pass at me or anything. So I kept on meeting him. And then—and then he proposed to me."

I nodded. "Sure. Only he couldn't marry you right off on account of his divorce wasn't final or something."

She looked startled. "How did you know?"

"It figures. So the two of you eloped, in a manner of speaking."

She bit her lip, nodded.

"On your money, I'd guess."

She nodded again. "I still have some left. He—he—" she broke off.

He hadn't been after her money was what she no doubt had been about to say. Naturally. Not with a face and figure like hers.

"Look," I said, "I'm not going to try and tell you this isn't the end of the world. It is, of course. And naturally you should kill yourself—it's the normal, healthy thing to do. But just as a hypothetical question, have you thought about chalking the whole thing up to experience and going back to your parents?"

She closed her eyes. "I couldn't. Not ever. Not after——"

"You're right," I said hastily. "Absolutely right. When they learned their daughter wasn't a virgin any more—something they may just possibly suspect already, by the way—the shock would upset them. I'm certain they'd be much happier to hear you were only dead. Then they could laugh the whole thing off."

She looked at me uncertainly. "I—I hadn't thought of

it that way. I—I guesss it would hurt them a lot more if I——"

"Uh uh," I said. "Don't start trying to back out of killing yourself now. You promised me you were going to kill yourself, and I'm going to see to it that you do—whether you want to or not. It's just a question of getting your motives clear. Now, you aren't going to kill yourself to make your parents happy—because it wouldn't have that effect. Right?"

She nodded, slowly.

"And you're not going to kill yourself to make your—your ex-lover *un*happy, because he most likely wouldn't ever know. Or care if he did know."

She nodded again, frowning.

"So obviously you're going to commit suicide to make *yourself* happy. Right? Sure. You've no idea how much better you'll feel when you're good and dead. It'll make a new woman of you."

I ordered another round. When it came we sipped in silence. It was her move, I figured.

"You're right," she said at last. "You're quite right." I said nothing, just sat and watched emotions move slowly across her face like cloud shadows on the desert. She was working things out in her mind, things she had to work out by herself. For a long time—or what seemed like a long time—I sat and watched her face and waited.

And then all of a sudden she smiled, a sad smile—but it was as if (if you'll pardon one more cliché) the sun had suddenly broken through the clouds.

"And I don't want to die," she said. "Not really. Not now I don't." She put her face in her hands and wept. But they weren't bitter tears. They were just—tears.

I slid around the table of the booth to sit beside her, put my arm around her shoulders, and let her weep.

The waiter glided up and studied us questioningly. I glared at him. He glided away.

For perhaps a full minute the two of us sat like that, she with her face buried in my shoulder, me with my hand gently stroking the long, copper-red waves of her hair.

Then she pulled herself away from me and smiled and took my handkerchief and dabbed at her eyes again.

"Thank you," she said. "Thank you—Jake? Is that what you said your name was?"

"Jake. Jake O'Day. And you're——?"

She hesitated. "Gretchen."

"Gretchen——?"

"Just—Gretchen. For now at least. All right?"

I nodded. The tiny purse that lay on the table before her had the initials G. J. on it. Jones? Johnson? It didn't matter. I'd find out in good time. It wouldn't do to rush things.

"Going back to your parents?" I asked.

She nodded, frowning. She looked suddenly like a schoolgirl. Which, undoubtedly, was what she was. She touched one finger to the moist edge of her glass, began to draw tiny wet circles on the shiny surface of the table.

"It's funny," she said. "It's almost funny. Just a few minutes ago I felt—I felt I couldn't bear to go on living. That I didn't want to live. And now——"

"Now you're a tiny bit drunk," I said. "Don't worry. You'll feel awful again when you sober up."

She blinked at me, smiled, then laughed. It was the first time I'd heard her laugh. I liked the sound.

"You're terrible," she said. "You say all the wrong things. But—but you say them nicely. Jake?"

"Yes?"

"I *am* going back to my parents. They'll shout at me and make me feel awful and all that—but I will go back. I won't—I won't kill myself. I really was going to you know."

"Yes," I said. "I know." Actually I figured that the chances had been about three to one against her killing herself even if she hadn't met me—but it wouldn't have been tactful to say so.

"As I said, I *will* go back. But Jake. I don't want to go back right away. Not today. I—I want just a little time to get the, the taste of—" She broke off and shivered a little. "I feel sort of unclean. Not because I'm not a virgin any more. I'm not all that silly. But it's not nice knowing that the first man—the only man—just took me and, well, *used* me. Do you understand how I feel?"

"Yes," I lied. How did she feel?

"I feel like I want to—to wash away the bad taste." She averted her eyes, bit her lip quickly. Even in the subdued light of the hotel bar I could see that she was blushing.

She laughed suddenly. A forced, artificial laugh. "I guess I am just a bit drunk. Only a little while ago I felt so wretched I didn't want to live. And now——"

She turned suddenly and looked me full in the eyes. It was like I'd been plugged in to a high-tension line, like I was suddenly floodlit inside. She was still blushing but she held my gaze. "Do you understand what I'm talking about, Jake?"

"Yes," I said, and I did. Fuses started popping all through my nervous system. A man had hurt her—and now she wanted a man to heal her. Me.

She closed her eyes tightly for a moment. When she spoke again her voice was almost a whisper. "We—I have a room here at the hotel. It's paid up to the end of the week. Jake. Jake, take me to my room. Please?"

She waited, eyes closed, for my answer. And for just a moment I hesitated. I wanted her right then more than I'd ever wanted any girl in my life. Because crazily, irrationally, I was in love with the frightened, bewildered, half-drunk schoolgirl by my side. But still I hesitated—for a moment.

Because while part of it was wonderfully right, part of it was horribly wrong. Because—crazily and irrationally—this was a girl I loved, a girl I thought of as my bride.

But she wasn't inviting me to her room and her arms as a husband. She was inviting me as a kind of emotional mouth wash. A likable ordinary guy she'd met who would serve to wipe away the sexual memory of a man she now hated.

So I hesitated. But only for a moment. What the hell, half the good things in life you get you get for the wrong reason.

"Let's go to your room," I said. And we went.

## Chapter 20

HER ROOM WAS SMALL by *Chez Cortes* standards, large by any other. The curtains were bottle-green and, drawn across the windows as they were that bright sunny afternoon, they flooded the room with bottle-green light.

It gave the entire room an odd, underwater appearance—like we were in some phantom undersea grotto. It was an eerie, rather pleasing effect, well in keeping with the somewhat drunken, somewhat dreamlike mood we both were in.

We stood for a moment staring at each other; both, for different—though not really so different—reasons a trifle ill at ease. A knock sounded at the door. It was the waiter, wheeling in the bottles of ice-cradled champagne I'd ordered. The waiter bustled in, uncorked one of the bottles, paused expectantly, was tipped, departed.

Again we sood facing each other; still awkward, still ill at ease.

"Drink?" I asked, pouring champagne into two glasses without waiting for her reply. She nodded. We drank. I poured again. We drank again, this time raising our glasses in a more than self-conscious toast.

"Look," I said when we'd drained our glasses. "If you've changed your mind—or if you want to change your mind——"

She shook her copper-red tresses, "Do it to me Jake. Please do it to me." Her creamy cheeks were again crimsoned but her eyes were steady pools of green fire. "Do it to me," she repeated. "Do it to me now."

I reached out and grasped her shoulders, shook her young body hard. At that moment I both loved and hated her—loved her because I couldn't help loving her, hated her because, in a way, she was merely using me as another man had used her.

"Say you love me," I shouted. "Tell me you love me."

"I love you," she repeated. "I love you Jake."

And I believed her. Perhaps because I wanted to believe her. But I believed her. I had to believe her.

"Take me," she gasped. "For the love of heaven take me Jake."

And I took her. She was trembling all over when I undressed her. I was more than a little unsteady myself, for that matter. I unwrapped her soft young body the way I'd unwrapped Christmas packages as a kid—slowly, so as to prolong the blissfully agonizing sensation of discovery. Slowly, almost reverently, I stripped her young body.

First the tiny bolero jacket she wore. Then the buttons running up the back of her blouse. The blouse slid floorward with a rustle of silk, exposing perfect creamy shoulders. Under the thin lace of her bra her breasts thrust tautly outward, high, firm, erect.

I found the bra's catch, loosened it, let the bra fall loose. Freed from the twin lace hammocks her breasts looked larger—but every bit as firm fleshed and high.

Her skirt was fastened by two buttons, a zipper. I unbuttoned and unzipped, let the skirt drop to a crumpled ring of cloth at her feet. Her body trembled a little as I hooked my fingers over the hem of her panties, pulled them slowly down over the creamy bowl of her stomach, the youthful flare of her hips.

Now she was nude save for her garter belt and stockings. My fingers kept working. Only stockings now.

I slid my fingers up the sleek, ripe fleshed sides of her thighs, gently rolled each stocking down, kissing each new inch of creamy flesh I uncovered.

She murmured softly in her throat.

I can barely remember stripping off my own clothes. All I can recall is that they seemed to drop as fast as snow slides off a tin roof. By the time I was completely naked she was lying on the bed, waiting.

Still she said nothing, but her eyes seemed to beckon to me, to shyly invite me to do as I wished—as we both wished.

I went to her, and we made love. Gently, slowly, tentatively; as if performing some age-old ritual exactly prescribed by tradition; as if we were both living in a dream world of slow motion.

I lay alongside of her and made love with my lips, my mouth pressing against hers, my tongue seeking the ripeness of her lips, the sweet tasting sanctuary of her mouth.

I made love with my fingertips, letting them trace lazy, dreamlike circles of spiralling desire over her shoulders, her breasts, her belly, her legs. I took my time. Even though my loins ached with the fervor of my desire I forced myself to move at a slow, unhurried pace, keeping my fingertips and tongue gliding over the creamy sculptured field of her body, seeking the sensitive, secret places of her body where my hands and lips would give her the most pleasure.

I kissed the hollow of her throat, the lobes of her ears, her eyelids, the nape of her neck.

I played her body as I might play a musical instrument, first tuning it, readying it, gently fingering from it the first tentative notes of response, of readiness.

Then I took her.

All her reserve had melted now; no longer was she a young girl shyly yielding herself to a lover—but a passion-drunk woman, a vessel of fiery lust, a frenzied, plunging, quivering, whimpering sex machine.

And then the warhead of our fused ecstasy exploded in a blinding, numbing, shattering multiple explosion of undreamed of delight. And it was over.

The spent rocket tumbled silently earthward through velvet darkness, the last glowing sparks of passion faded gently into oblivion. And by and by I could see and hear and think again.

I thought how strange—and yet how wonderful—that I should fall so completely in love with a girl who's very existence I'd been unaware of an hour ago.

I heard the soft, rhythmic whisper of her breathing, and it was music to my ears. I opened my eyes and saw the splendor of her flaming hair, the perfection of her youthful face. And I was content.

Content hell, I was punch drunk with happiness. I was on top of the world.

## Chapter 21

I DON'T KNOW how long I slept, but when I woke darkness had fallen over Mexico City. And over me. And Gretchen.

Gretchen. I turned, lazily, contentedly on the bed and reached out for her. She wasn't there.

I sat up abruptly, looked around the darkened room. She was gone.

I got up, snapped on a light. No suitcase, no clothes in the closet. I picked up the phone, called the desk.

The lady in room 412? She had checked out an hour ago. No, no forwarding address. In fact—the clerk hesitated—in fact the lady specifically stated that if anyone should ask where she could be reached, he should be told that the lady did not wish to be reached.

I hung up.

Then I swore. For about fifteen minutes straight I swore. Why in hell was I such a heavy sleeper? Why hadn't I awakened when she'd gotten up and dressed?

I could have talked to her, reasoned with her.

Damn. A million times damn. I hadn't even told her I loved her. Maybe she thought she was just another quick conquest to me, another notch to cut in my belt.

Did she think that? What had she thought when she'd awakened alone in the dark with a strange man by her side? That I was the comic ending to a week of grand tragedy? An amusing episode?

No. No, that couldn't be. Surely. Surely I hadn't imagined that sudden startled flash of awareness in her eyes when we'd first met. Miserable and unhappy though she'd been, she too must have sensed that spark passing between us, linking us.

I reached for the open bottle of champagne—untasted, now flat—and took a swig. Maybe I was just a sentimentalist. After all, just because I had fallen instantly in love was no indication that— Nuts.

Still, it hurt that she hadn't left so much as a *thank you* note. Still swearing I pulled on my clothes. Then I glanced into a mirror—and smiled. She had left a species of *thank you* note: in the middle of my forehead was the lipstick imprint of her lips.

Foolishly, irrationally, my hopes soared again. I could find her. It shouldn't be too hard. Where had she and her parents been? Acapulco. Doubtless they—and she—wouldn't be there now, but back wherever they lived in the States.

But I could trace her. Some hotel clerk in Acapulco would remember a girl with creamy skin and copper-red hair, a girl whose first name was Gretchen and whose last name began with J.

I could— Hell, I couldn't. Not yet. I had Sam on my hands.

I finished dressing and went back to our suite. Sam

wasn't there. I looked in his bedroom to see if he'd left a note or something. He had.

*Dear Jake*, read the note. *While you were out the Armenian telephoned. His voice sounded funny, like he was disguising it. He said he'd been observing us to see if we measured up. He said I measured up. He said you didn't, though, on account of you drink too much and chase girls all the time. Hence he's hiring me instead of you. Tough break for you. So long, it's been instructive knowing you. Sam.*

I grabbed for the telephone and asked for long distance.

"Why in hell," I demanded when Barnaby answered his phone, "did you write me out of the plot? What kind of a double-cross are you trying to pull, anyway?"

"Huh?" said Barnaby. "Explain yourself."

I explained myself.

"Incredible," said Barnaby. "Somebody is tampering with our plot."

"You mean you didn't call Sam in a disguised voice?"

"Certainly not. I don't even have the rest of your adventure worked out, in fact. Curious. Most curious. I wonder who *did* call. Perhaps some editor vacationing at the same hotel—editors never can resist monkeying with other people's plots."

"Don't make jokes," I snarled. "Don't you realize what's happened? Someone's stolen Sam."

"Ridiculous. Why would anyone want to steal Sam?"

He had a point there. Why *would* anyone— I stopped. "Barnaby," I said slowly, "what if he's been kidnaped? His old man is worth three-quarters of a billion bucks, you know."

"It's an angle," Barnaby agreed. "A potent angle. Not my kind of plot, but—yeah, it's a distinct possibility. Let me think. How would someone work a caper like that? Hmm. Couldn't put the snatch on him at the hotel obviously. So the thing to do is lure Sam off some place—then hold him for ransom. Yeah, that's most likely what's happened. Most any day now his father will start getting ransom notes, probably accompanied by some of Sam's fingers for identification purposes."

I felt sick. "Barnaby," I said, "we've got to find him.

If I louse up this job his old man will see I never get another."

"That's the kind of practical, cold-blooded approach I admire," said Barnaby. "But finding him may not be easy. He may not even be in Mexico City. A sensible kidnaper would lure him off to some small town before kidnaping him."

"Don't just think up complications," I pleaded. "Do something constructive."

Barnaby muttered annoyance. "Do I have to do *all* the thinking? Yes, I guess I do. Jiggle the phone."

"Huh?"

"Jiggle the phone button," repeated Barnaby patiently, "so's to get the hotel operator on the line."

I did so. She asked what we wanted. "We want," said Barnaby, "to know if a young man with pimples on his face made inquiries about plane tickets. Or bus tickets. Or train tickets."

"Yes," said the hotel operator a few minutes later. "A plane ticket to Tampico."

"There," said Barnaby triumphantly. "Now all you have to do is hop a plane in pursuit. Uh, let me know how things work out."

He hung up.

Damn the man. He had things easy—authors always did: their characters did their dirty work for them.

I called the desk and made a reservation for the first plane to Tampico and started hurling things into my suitcase.

## Chapter 22

TAMPICO AIRPORT SMELLED VAGUELY—and inexplicably—of banana oil mixed with sweat. It was also hot as hell. I took a taxi and told the driver to take me to the best hotel in town. Either the taxi driver lacked judgment or Tampico's best left a lot to be desired.

I took a large room with telephone and called Barnaby.

"I've arrived in Tampico," I informed him. "How do I go about finding Sam?"

"Mmmm," said Barnaby. "Let me think."

"Think fast," I snapped. "Sam may be in bad shape by now."

"Did you try the obvious things—like calling all the hotels in town?"

"No," I said. "Stay by the phone, I'll call you back."

I cradled the phone and went downstairs to locate the hotel phone operator. She proved to be an almond-eyed young chick with bedroom eyes and picture window cleavage.

"I want you to do me a favor," I told her, piling pesos in front of her.

"With much pleasure, señor," she said, stuffing the pesos down the front of her dress. "I am off duty in half an hour and——"

"Not that kind of a favor," I said. "I'm looking for a young American, a boy."

She shrugged. "To each his own. But must you have an American boy? There are many fine Mexican youths in Tampico who cater to——"

"This is business," I snarled. "I want you to call every hotel and boarding house in town, find out if a jerk named Sam Tamerlane has checked in. He may not have used his own name, so ask them if an American boy of about eighteen with pimples has checked in."

"As you wish, señor."

"And right away," I said, stuffing another pile of pesos into the front of her dress.

"Certainly. But if your need is so urgent, perhaps one of the bellboys——"

"No!" I yelled. Back upstairs I had time to take a leisurely shower and down three gin and tonics before she called back.

"No luck señor. Perhaps, just this once, you would consider a young girl such as myself?"

"Maybe later. Now get me long distance again. Malibu, California."

"The obvious didn't work," I told Barnaby when he answered. "Think of something else."

"Hum. Well, in one of the *Dirk Dagger* shows, *Quell Me In Quebec* it was called, I had Dirk hire all the taxi drivers in town to act as spies."

"Good," I said. "What else?"

"Well, in *I, Smuggler*—a C movie I wrote last year—the hero located his man through a street photographer. You know, one of those guys who stand on street corners taking pictures of tourists and handing out tickets so that——"

"I know, I know," I snarled. "I saw the movie, come to think of it. What else?"

"That's all I can think of right now. I'll have a look through some of my old scripts, though."

"Do that," I said, and hung up.

In front of the hotel I found four or five taxi drivers standing around. It took me ten minutes to convince them that I was more interested in finding a pimple-faced American boy than in sampling the virginity of anybody's sister, but finally—spurred on by the five hundred peso bonus I offered—they agreed to pass the word among the taxi drivers of Tampico.

"Fine," I said. "If any of them has a fare even remotely resembling an eighteen-year-old American boy with pimples I want to know about it. Now, is there a street photographer in town?"

They looked blank. "Photographer. You know—pictures."

"Ah!" they chorused. "Sí. Pablo. We will take you to him."

"One of you will take me to him," I corrected. "The rest will spread the word that I'm looking for Sam."

Pablo proved to be the proprietor of a tiny, dingy camera shop wedged in between a taxidermist's and a pawnbroker. Both the shop and Pablo—who boasted the largest handle-bar moustache I'd ever seen—were marvelously sinister. It was too bad Sam wasn't along to soak in the atmosphere.

"Señor?" inquired Pablo beaming at me from behind the counter.

"This gringo wishes to look at your pictures," said the taxi driver who'd brought me.

"But certainly. Bolt the door, Pepe." Pablo reached under the counter and produced a thick stack of glossy prints. He spread them lovingly on the counter before me.

"Enticing, no? If Pablo says so himself, there are no filthier pictures in all Tampico—in all Mexico."

"Wow!" I said. "You're not kidding." I tore my eyes away from the prints with difficulty. "But I'm not interested in pictures like this—not right now, anyway. What I want to see is all the pictures you've taken on the street recently."

"The street? But señor, one does not take pictures like these on the street. You understand the police here are most tolerant—two, three, four naked señoritas posing on the sidewalk—they would merely shrug. But the señoritas would be shy—many come from the best families and——"

"I mean pictures of tourists. With clothes on. I want to see all the pictures you or your assistants have taken of American tourists in the last few hours."

Pablo beamed and said he understood perfectly—which I doubted—and that I had indeed come to the right place: although he, Pablo, did not waste his time taking pictures of tourists, most of the street photographers in Tampico brought their films to him to develop. "Because I am the best man in a dark room in all Tampico," he confided. "Also I work cheap." His face fell. "But I have not developed today's pictures yet. You will come back?"

I piled pesos on the counter. "I will wait. And the less time I wait the more generous I will feel."

Twenty minutes later, after another pile of pesos had changed hands, Pablo handed me a pile of still damp prints. I looked through them hastily. A group of obvious schoolteachers. A fat lady with dark glasses. A tourist couple with two small children. More schoolteachers. Another family group of tourists. A thin woman walking a fat dog. And then I was staring at a familiar if somewhat blurred figure.

"Ah ha!" said Pablo. "You have found your man, eh?"

"No," I said. "And then again, maybe yes." I peered at the blurred picture again. In the background was a whitewashed building that seemed vaguely familiar.

"Where would this have been taken?" I asked.

Pablo and the taxi driver peered at the print. "At the airport," said the taxi driver. "Too bad," added Pablo. "If it had been taken in front of a hotel you would know where your friend was staying, no?"

I nodded. I handed the print back to Pablo and began

piling more pesos in front of him. "Make a whole lot of copies of this," I told him. I turned to the taxi driver and began counting out more pesos. "And when he gets 'em made up, I want you to distribute a copy to every taxi driver in town. Tell them I'll pay a thousand pesos to locate this bird."

"Sí. And how does this one call himself?"

"Probably Jones or Smith," I said. "But back in California he called himself James T. Quinn."

Ten minutes later I was back in my hotel and on the phone to Walter C. Tamerlane. He seemed delighted to hear from me. "How's the adventure going, O'Day?" A hearty chuckle. "My boy getting a lot of cloak and dagger nonsense out of his system?"

"Yeah," I said, "he's having the time of his life." And no doubt he was. If he was alive that is.

"You boys are certainly having a grand tour," continued Mr. Tamerlane. "Trinidad, Mexico City, and now where are you?"

"In trouble," I said. "I mean Tampico. How did you know we were in Trinidad and then Mexico City?"

"Why, through that writer fellow you hired, of course. You told him to clear all expenses through Quinn."

"Yeah," I agreed, "so I did. By the way, where is your assistant right now?"

"Home I expect. Left the office yesterday complaining about an upset stomach. Didn't come in today. Why do you ask?"

"Idle curiosity. How about Dr. Bolingbrook—he around?"

"Who no, as it happens. Left yesterday for some convention. Clever fellow, Bolingbrook. Full of bright ideas."

"Yeah. How did you happen to hire him as your personal psychologist, by the way?"

"Why—I believe Quinn ran across him."

"Uh huh. And how, may I ask, did you happen to hire Quinn?"

A beefy chuckle. "Nepotism, sheer nepotism. He's not a close relative but——"

I didn't hear the rest. Someone was pounding on my hotel door. "Call you back," I yelled. I cradled the phone and leaped to open the door.

It was the taxi driver who'd taken me to Pablo's. He beamed at me. "An amazing coincidence," he told me. "I have found both the men you seek—also one extra gringo. Fifteen hundred pesos, please."

"Where?"

"Ah ha. That would be telling. First you give me the fifteen hundred pesos, *then* I tell you where to find them."

I dug frantically through my pockets. Damn. I was getting low on currency.

"Thirteen, fourteen hundred pesos," said the taxi driver, counting what I'd thrust into his palms. "You are a hundred pesos short. No matter. I shall wait while you cash a check downstairs at the desk. No doubt you have travelers' checks? Or perhaps you can wire for funds. It should not take more than——"

"Here," I snarled, handing him my wrist watch, "it's worth more than a hundred pesos."

The taxi driver inspected my watch closely, then nodded. "Sí. I will take you to where I saw your friends now. But I do not think there is any hurry, señor. Most likely they are all dead by now." He winked at me. "That, señor, is why I asked to be paid in advance. Shrewd, no?"

## Chapter 23

WHILE THE TAXI DRIVER, the taxi and I hurtled through the darkening streets of Tampico the taxi driver told me how he'd happened to locate Sam.

"It was, señor, a miraculous stroke of luck. Fate, you might say, smiled upon me." He wrenched the wheel and we skidded around a hairpin corner on two wheels. "As I was saying," he continued after my scream of panic had died away, "it was destiny. I was just leaving Pablo's with the photographs to distribute, you know?"

I said I did and closed my eyes as the taxi screeched between a brick wall and a wildly honking truck.

"When who should stop my cab but a gringo with a beard—a long white beard."

"A what?"

"A beard. To continue, this bearded gringo jumps into my taxi, glances at a piece of paper in his hand, and then commands me to take him to the warehouse on Diablo Blanco wharf. This, I say to myself, is very strange—because there is no ship tied up at Diablo Blanco wharf, and the warehouse is, as you say, deserted."

The taxi driver turned and smiled at me. "But that is not all that is strange."

"Watch the road!" I yelled.

The driver nodded and turned back in time to skid the taxi around the wrong side of an on-coming bus. "As I was saying, this is not all that is strange. This gringo who wishes to go to the warehouse on Diablo Blanco wharf has a long white beard—but his face is very young. With pimples."

"Sam!"

"Sí. I say to myself. It is the lost young American in a lousy disguise."

"And you took him to the warehouse?"

"I did. He pays me and tells me to drive away. Which I do—but slowly. I wish to see if he goes into the warehouse, so I can report to you and make five hundred pesos."

"And he went in? Alone?"

"Sí. But a moment later two other gringos tiptoe in after him. One is the man whose picture you found at Pablo's, the other is one I do not know—a funny little man with a big bald head and glasses."

I cursed to myself. Dr. Bolingbrook and Quinn.

"Okay," I said to the taxi driver, "you earned your money all right. But why do you think they're all dead by now?"

"Because, señor, but a moment after they all have gone into the warehouse, much shooting breaks in—I correct myself—breaks out. I do not stay to see if there are any survivors but drive straight to your hotel."

The taxi was careening along the waterfront now, past brightly lighted ships to our right and bars to our left. Then the lights began to thin out and a few minutes later the road was pitch dark save for the taxi's headlights and a bilious looking quarter moon glittering on the water.

"Not far now," said the driver. "Another mile perhaps."

I spent the last mile fuming. James T. Quinn. James Tamerlane Quinn, undoubtedly. A relative but not a close one, Mr. Tamerlane had said. But if Sam was out of the way—like dead—even an un-close relative would be the logical heir to the family business. Quinn had already worked his way up to the number two spot—how it must have bugged him every time Walter C. talked about turning Tamerlane Oil over to Sam.

Yeah, it should have been obvious right from the start. Not to *me*—this sort of thing wasn't my line—but it should have been obvious to Barnaby. Plots were his business. If Barnaby had had his wits about him he'd have figured out the whole scheme right off the bat.

Quinn needed Sam out of the way—but any kind of skulduggery was out of the question with Sam living in a fortress like Tamerlane Castle. So Quinn had brought in another crook, Dr. Bolingbrook, and Bolingbrook had talked the old man into providing his son with a "controlled adventure," an adventure they intended should get out of control just long enough for Sam to wind up dead.

And who'd have gotten the blame? Barnaby and I, that's who. Already I could hear the prosecutor's sneering voice as he wound up his case:

*Can any intelligent member of the jury believe for one minute that the death of young Sam Tamerlane—whose frail bullet ridden body was found in a warehouse in Tampico—can any member of the jury believe his untimely death was an "accident?"*

*Of course not! Directly or indirectly, Sam Tamerlane was murdered by the two defendants you see cringing before you: a cold-blooded soldier of fortune whose brutal fame has spread throughout the civilized world—and a cold-blooded writer who has broken down under questioning and admitted he gets a big kick out of knocking off his characters.*

*I submit, ladies and gentlemen, that this cold-blooded writer, when he turned to plotting a real life drama, decided he'd get an even bigger kick out of knocking off a real human being—and Jake of Arabia was only too happy to oblige!*

(Crys of "No! No!" from Barnaby and me—instantly drowned out by jeers and boos from the judge and jury.)

*Remember, ladies and gentlemen of the jury, these two fiends have admitted they hired men to shoot at young Sam, to terrorize him. Hence it matters little whether they actually meant to finish off the poor boy then and there—or whether one of their trigger-happy hirelings misjudged his aim and sent his bullets crashing into young Sam instead of past his innocent head.*

*In either case Jake and Barnaby are responsible—and I demand the death penalty!*

I shivered. Hell, if anybody summed up the caper like that *I'd* vote myself the death penalty. Fiends like Barnaby and I shouldn't be allowed to run around loose.

"It is just ahead, señor," said the taxi driver, slowing the taxi to a cautious halt. He'd already turned out the headlights, and looming ahead of us in the semi-darkness I could clearly make out the silhouette of a long, one-story warehouse. In the moonlight it looked ominous as hell—like a set for an Alfred Hitchcock mystery.

The two of us got out and advanced slowly on foot. "All seems quiet now," whispered the taxi driver. "But only a little while ago——"

A brief volley of shots broke out inside the warehouse.

The taxi driver gave a squeak of panic and turned and dashed back towards his taxi. Fear lent speed to his feet; he ran so fast he almost overtook me.

Seconds later the two of us stuck our heads cautiously around the rear of the taxi. All was quiet again.

"You are going in to rescue your friend, no?" asked the taxi driver.

"No," I said automatically. But at that moment someone flipped a switch inside the warehouse, flooding the darkness with light. The top of the warehouse had glass sky-lights along most of its length, making the whole top look like an illuminated green house.

Evidently things were sufficiently decided one way or another so that someone felt safe enough in turning on the lights. Also, all that light inside would make it tough for anyone in the warehouse to see anyone outside. So I decided to risk taking a quick peek.

I reached the wall of the warehouse without making any more noise than a mouse walking over cotton wool and almost immediately found a ladder. I climbed up it.

Now I was on the roof itself, peering down through

the skylight. I inched myself cautiously forward. Voices.

"Give up, Sam. We know you're out of ammunition. We heard your gun click." Quinn's voice.

"Yes, my boy. Further resistance would indeed be immature. Come out and permit us to despatch you quickly and humanely." Dr. Bolingbrook.

I took a precarious hand hold and leaned forward a little more. All at once I could see Sam, white false beard askew, crouching behind an old oil drum. He was clutching his gun in one hand. Evidently he'd gotten some live cartridges for it. Evidently he hadn't gotten enough—as I watched he aimed it and pulled the trigger. I distinctly heard the empty click it made.

"He's over there!" said Quinn's voice—and at that moment he and Dr. Bolingbrook, guns leveled, came into view directly beneath me. "You're finished, Sam," gloated Quinn. "You haven't a chance!"

I studied the situation. He was right. Poor Sam. Nothing could save him now. I started to turn away. Much though I disliked Sam as a person, I couldn't bear to watch him being riddled with bullets. It would give me nightmares later. And there was really nothing that I could do, save tiptoe silently——

And at that moment my foot slipped . . .

## Chapter 24

"AMAZING," SAID BARNABY some days later as I sat lounging in his beach house filling in various details for him. "You say you hurled yourself feet first through the skylight, bellowing defiance at the killers below you?"

"Well, more or less," I said modestly. Actually I'd been screaming with fear, but I saw no point in filling Barnaby in on *all* the details. "However I must admit that it was partly luck that my right foot hit Dr. Bolingbrook on the back of his head while my left knocked Quinn cold."

"And the fall knocked you out too, you say?"

"Right. When I came to Sam was bending over me, false beard and all—and Quinn and Dr. Bolingbrook had vanished."

"Vanished where?"

"I thought it best not to inquire," I admitted. "If I had, Sam might have told me. Of course, it's quite possible Sam revived them and told them to go away and sin no more. On the other hand—" On the other hand the warehouse had been only a few feet from the dark waters of the Gulf of Mexico. And the tide had been going out.

"You were right not to inquire," Barnaby agreed. "After all, they were killers, or would-be killers. But what I can't understand is why Sam—after such a successful first caper—should decide to come back to take over his father's oil business. It just doesn't make sense—profitable though his decision was to you."

"Sure it makes sense," I said. "Sam had grown up thinking of his father's business as dull. The idea that anybody would try to kill him just to take over Tamerlane Oil intrigued him. For the first time he realized that big business sometimes involves the scientific application of force.

"Naturally I encouraged this idea—pointed out how in the old days oil companies had pioneered in the use of imaginative violence—crushing small competitors, blowing up rival companies' pipe lines, blackmailing Arab sheiks into signing concessions. Sam pratically wept for joy at the thought of doing likewise. I suspect," I added, "that Sam may turn out to be the last and toughest of the robber barons."

Barnaby nodded and got up to pour us a fresh round of drinks. "When Sam gets in the saddle of Tamerlane Oil," he mused, "Heaven help Standard Oil and Royal Dutch Shell."

We drank in silence.

"And what are you going to do now?" Barnaby asked. "Spend your fifty-thousand-dollar bonus on women and wine?"

"Buy an airplane, I guess. Start an air taxi service. If I'm my own boss nobody can fire me on account of my past. But not right away. First I've got to make a quick trip to Acapulco. Which reminds me, if you knew only the first name and last initial of a girl, how would you go about—" I stopped.

"Yes?" said Barnaby leaning forward eagerly. "A new real life adventure for me to manipulate?"

I got to my feet and shook my head. "Thanks just the same, Barnaby. But all things considered, I think I'll plot my own life from now on."

"Suit yourself," said Barnaby. "But if you need any help—like an exciting climax or anything—let me know."

"Don't worry," I said, "when I find her I'll bring things to a climax myself. Metaphorically speaking, that is."

And metaphorically speaking, I did.

# TO THE READER

If you enjoyed this book, you will be glad to know that there are many others just as well written, just as interesting, to be had in the Fiction House Press Library.

You will find the Fiction House Press Library online at

www.FictionHousePress.com

www.ingramcontent.com/pod-product-compliance
Lightning Source LLC
LaVergne TN
LVHW091006080826
845145LV00003B/1157

* 9 7 8 1 6 4 7 2 0 2 3 3 0 *